Destiny's Kiss

Prequel to the
Legendary Bastards of the Crown Series

By

Elizabeth Rose

RoseScribe Media Inc
Cover by Dar Albert & Elizabeth Rose Krejcik
Edited by Scott Moreland

ISBN – 13: 978-1541309289
ISBN – 10: 1541309286

Books by Elizabeth Rose:

♛ (Legacy of the Blade Series)
♛ Prequel
♛ Lord of the Blade – Book 1
♛ Lady Renegade – Book 2
♛ Lord of Illusion – Book 3
♛ Lady of the Mist – Book 4

♝ (Daughters of the Dagger Series)
♝ Prequel
♝ Ruby – Book 1
♝ Sapphire – Book 2
♝ Amber – Book 3
♝ Amethyst – Book 4

♜ (MadMan MacKeefe Series)
♜ Onyx – Book 1
♜ Aidan – Book 2
♜ Ian – Book 3

✳ (Elemental Series)
✳ The Dragon and the DreamWalker: Book 1, Fire
✳ The Duke and the Dryad: Book 2, Earth
✳ The Sword and the Sylph: Book 3, Air
✳ The Sheik and the Siren: Book 4, Water

♞ (Greek Myth Fantasy)
♞ Kyros' Secret
♞ The Oracle of Delphi
♞ Thief of Olympus
♞ The Pandora Curse

And More!
Visit http://elizabethrosenovels.com

Author's Note:

This is the prequel of the Legendary Bastards of the Crown Series.

It is followed by the stories of the three boys after they are grown.

Restless Sea Lord – Book 1 (Rowen the Restless)
Ruthless Knight – Book 2 (Rook the Ruthless)
Reckless Highlander – Book 3 (Reed the Reckless)

Chapter 1

England, 1344

Ross of Clan Douglas lifted his tankard, watching the English messenger of King Edward III with intent. Ross' brother, Malcolm, and his two good friends, Breac and Niven, occupied a table at the Devil's Eye with him. The Devil's Eye was a border tavern run by the English who happened to befriend some of the Lowland Scots, Clan Douglas included.

"I wonder what brings Edward's men in here," he said, setting down his tankard. His eyes were still fastened on the king's messenger and two English guards sitting at a table across the room.

"This could be our chance," said Malcolm, leaning over and speaking to his brother in a low voice. The tavern was noisy and busy. A traveling musician plucked a lively tune on a lute from the opposite side of the room. Bonnie serving wenches hustled back and forth bringing customers tankards of ale, whisky, and wine.

"Ye have been waitin' to pay back Edward for what he did to yer family," said Niven with a nod of his head. "Mayhap, this is yer chance."

"Go, find out," said Breac.

"Ye fools, I canna just walk up and ask them." Ross studied the serving wench, Ella, who spoke to the Englishmen at their table, taking their orders. Ella was Ross' favorite serving girl and he'd had her on several occasions. She was a Lowlander like him and not English. Ella would also do anything for Ross. Perhaps she'd overheard something at the Englishmen's table. He had to find out.

The Devil's Eye was often inhabited by both the English and the Scots. Lowlanders had quite a different relationship with the English on this side of the border than the Highlanders who were not accepted in mixed company. Pushing up from his chair, he made his way over to the opposite end of the room where a kissing bough hung from a beam in the ceiling, being placed there in the spirit of Christmas, bringing joy to the patrons who had a chance to kiss a wench or two in fun.

"Ella," he said and the girl stopped beneath the bough. He glanced back over to the table with the Englishmen. Then he pulled her into his arms and kissed her passionately on the mouth.

"Ross, no' now," she scolded. "I am workin' or didna ye notice?"

"I did," he said, leaning over and whispering into her ear. "Tell me. Why is the king's messenger here and where is he goin'?"

"I overheard them sayin' somethin' about takin' a missive to Hetherpool Castle," she whispered back.

"Hetherpool?" he asked, in confusion. "Why?"

"I dinna ken," she answered. "Now leave me be, Ross. I have to get the Englishmen their drinks."

Ross glanced over his shoulder, seeing the king's messenger putting a folded parchment into a pouch that sat on the floor by his feet. He needed to know what the missive said and would do anything to find out. He'd spent too many years trying to avenge King Edward for the raids that took most the members of their clan as well as his family. The only blood relative that had survived was his brother, Malcolm, who hated the English just as much as he did.

Ross strolled over to the drink board where Ella collected tankards of ale. "Keep the Englishmen's drinks comin' all night," he said, tossing a few coppers onto the tray she used. "And bring them no' only ale but also some of the finest Scottish whisky."

"That whisky is potent and the English dinna usually drink it," exclaimed Ella. "Ross? What are ye doin'? And shall I tell them who sent them the drinks?"

"Nay, dinna say a word." He looked over to the Englishmen once more. "There is somethin' I'd like ye to do for me, Ella." He took another coin from the sporran tied to his waist and pushed it into her palm. "Once they are well in their cups, I need ye to steal the missive from the messenger's pouch."

"Nay!" She pushed the coin back at him. He pulled her into his arms and kissed her deeply. Taking his mouth from hers, he noticed she'd closed her eyes during the kiss and he knew now he could convince her to do anything. "I'll make it worth yer while, Ella. I need to see what is in that missive."

"I could get killed if they catch me stealin' it," she protested, shaking her head at him.

"I willna let that happen." He reached for his sword fastened to his side to prove his point. "My brother and two of my friends will act on my orders. I'll be sure to protect ye from the bastards if trouble arises." He took the coin and placed it in her cleavage as her breasts were trussed up enticingly. If he didn't have other things on his mind right now, he might have considered taking her out to the stables and rewarding her before she even accomplished the mission.

"All right, I'll do it for ye," she said, letting out a sigh. "But dinna ever ask me to do somethin' like this again."

"I promise. Never again." He ran a finger over her cheek. "Thank ye, Ella."

Ross made his way back to the table where his friends waited anxiously. He never took his eyes off the Englishmen.

"How much longer?" complained Niven.

"Why dinna ye just go steal it yerself?" asked Breac.

"Hush," said Ross, silencing his friends. "If we get anywhere near their table, it's goin' to alarm them. Ella will deliver. Just give her time."

Sure enough, two hours later, the Englishmen looked to be well in their cups. He saw Ella glance back at him and Ross nodded, giving her the signal. She leaned over the table to collect the empty tankards and, at the same time, her other hand slipped down into the messenger's pouch, snagging the missive. She cleverly hid the parchment in her hand that was holding the tray.

"Here she comes," said Malcolm, as if they needed the announcement.

"Dinna raise suspicion," Ross warned, just as anxious as the others to know what message the king was sending to Hetherpool. "All of ye, look away from their table."

"I canna believe what I do for ye," complained Ella, walking over and dropping the missive onto Ross' lap.

"Ye are the best, Ella," he said, fingering the parchment under the table. Ella scowled and headed away.

"What is it?" asked Niven, trying to see the letter.

"Look at yer drinks only," he warned, glancing down to his lap to see the king's seal embossed into the wax keeping the missive closed. He carefully used his fingernail to lift the wax on the edges, managing to open the letter without breaking the seal in the least.

"Hurry up," Malcolm told him. "We need to get out of here before they discover it is gone."

Ross' eyes scanned the missive as he read the king's words. A smile lit up his face.

"What does it say?" asked Niven, his eyes skimming the edge of the table.

"It looks like we've got our lucky break," answered Ross. "The king's mistress is about to give birth. Edward says he'll be joinin' her in Hetherpool soon and hopes to get there before the bastard is born."

"How is that lucky?" grumbled Malcolm. He reached around a burning candle in the center of the table to pick up a pitcher of ale to pour himself another drink.

"We're goin' to alter this missive. When the Lord of Hetherpool receives it, it'll say the king wants naught to do with his mistress and bastard and that he's sent someone to marry the girl and make an alliance with her father, instead." Ross felt satisfied with this idea, but he should have known the others wouldn't accept the plan so easily.

"What are ye sayin'?" asked Niven. "Who are ye talkin' about?"

"Me," said Ross with a grin.

"Ye're addled, brathair," grumbled Malcolm. "Ye'll never get away with it."

"I will as long as I can convince Ella to find me a quill and some ink. The tavern owner should have some in the back room."

"If the king's seal is broken, no one will believe the missive," spat Breac.

"I've learned to open a missive without breakin' a seal," Ross told them with pride, his eyes landing on the burning red candle in the center of the table and the wax dripping down over the edges of the bottle that held it steady. "I'll just write a new letter and add more wax to hold the king's seal in place. No one will even ken it's been tampered with. I'll have Ella sneak it back into the messenger's pouch and he'll deliver it for us. We'll show up at the castle's gate right afterward and be welcomed with open arms."

"What will ye write?" asked Malcolm. "I dinna understand yer fool idea."

"I will do all I can to get back at Edward. I will start by takin' from him no' only his mistress but his bastard child as well." Ross folded the missive on his lap, running his finger over the wax seal in thought.

Niven almost choked on his ale and Breac's eyes opened wide at hearing Ross' words.

"Do ye think we can pull this off?" asked Breac.

"I can and I will. I'll tamper with Edward's words to make it read that he no longer wants the wench and the bairn, and that he's arranged for an alliance and husband for the girl, instead."

"And that would be ye?" asked Malcolm.

"The one and only," Ross answered with a devious grin.

"It's a suicide mission is what it is," snapped Malcolm. "We'll never get away with it and ye ken I'm right."

"It's a chance I'm willin' to take," said Ross, feeling vengeance pushing through his veins, driving him forward. "Edward took everythin' from us and we'll just be repayin' the favor. Now we just need to make sure we get Lord Ramsay Granville of Hetherpool to agree to the weddin' as soon as possible. We'll sweep the wench out of there as fast as we can and be halfway back to Scotland before the king even shows his face at the castle's gate."

"I dinna ken about this foolishness," said Niven.

"Neither do I," added Breac.

"I'll go alone if I have to, but I'd prefer if the three of ye were there with me to watch my back." There was an awkward pause of silence before Ross' friends answered.

"All right," Niven finally agreed, cradling the tankard in his hands. "I'll do it."

"So will I," added Breac, fidgeting nervously. "Ye've always been there for me, Ross, and I willna let ye down."

"What about ye, Malcolm?" Ross looked over to his brother who stared down into his tankard of ale in deep thought. He lifted it to his mouth, downed the contents, and slammed the vessel down atop the worn wood. His eyes traveled back to the table of Englishmen and, slowly, the corners of his mouth turned up into a grin.

"I like it and am only angry I didna think of it first," he said. They all started laughing. "I'm there for ye, brathair. Now, get that servin' wench back here quickly. We have work to do. This is one mission I'm more than willin' to risk my life for and only wish I could see Edward's face when he finds out a Scot has stolen his mistress and his bastard!"

Chapter 2

Lady Annalyse Granville was sure to go straight to hell. Clad in her plain, rough-hewn brown gown with her head covered by a white wimple, she clutched her long woolen cloak around her body, shivering from the winter cold. Purposely pausing in the entranceway of her father's great hall, she'd stopped directly under the holy bough – or what was known to many as the kissing bough.

Having been raised in the abbey although she wasn't a nun, Annalyse shared the morals and customs of the women of the cloth but hated every minute of it. However, even with her sheltered life she was wise to the legends of the kissing bough and knew that any lady standing under it from Christmastide all the way to Twelfth Night would receive a kiss, or perhaps several, from any knight or passing lord.

Most noblewomen her age were already married or at least betrothed. Annalyse was twenty years of age and, sadly, had never even experienced a kiss from a man. This was because of her curse of being born the second twin – a position that tagged her as a spawn of the devil. The consequences of her birth made her feared and undesirable to everyone. Of course, it was naught but an addlepated superstition, but her father believed it. That is why she'd been sent to live with the nuns. No one wanted their life cursed by an evil second-born twin bringing them bad luck. Matter of fact, no one wanted a second-born twin at all.

She hated superstition since it ruined her life. If it hadn't been for her ill luck, she'd be here celebrating Christmas with the rest of her family, as was her right for being born a noble. But instead of being treated with respect and honor for being the noblewoman she truly was, others acted as if she had the plague and went out of their way to avoid her.

If the nuns had known of her whereabouts tonight, they would tell her she had no right to be in a hall full of knights that were all well in their cups on this cold winter's eve. Annalyse shook her head. It no longer mattered because she didn't care. Her presence here tonight was for a reason. Her twin sister, Gabrielle, had sent her a missive and it had sounded so urgent that she'd daringly sneaked out of the abbey and traveled unescorted to the borderlands during the night so she wouldn't let her sister down. Her actions tonight had been dangerous, reckless, and bold, and it hadn't stopped with her journey here.

Looking up to the kissing bough hanging right above her head, her heartbeat resounded in her ears so loudly she was sure others could hear it, too. Never had she thought she'd ever be standing under a kissing bough and the idea excited her. The bough was a ball interwoven with twigs and fir tree greenery, decorated with an apple, candles, and berries. The abundance of holly decorating it would surely bring good luck.

Then she saw the ivy above her head and a knot formed in her stomach. Everyone knew ivy was supposed to be kept outdoors and not brought across the threshold because that meant death. Then again, perhaps that was naught more than a silly superstition. Dangling precariously from the bottom of the kissing bough was a fresh sprig of green mistletoe with several small, white berries. This was something she'd never seen at the abbey. The church didn't allow mistletoe within its holy walls since it was associated with pagan customs and Druids.

Once again, Annalyse felt as if she were doing something naughty by standing here. Not just because of the traditions, but because her sister needed her and she was purposely stalling. Gabrielle, being the first-born twin, had experienced kisses under the mistletoe many times in her life and Annalyse decided now it was her turn. She couldn't pass up this opportunity. Even though Gabrielle was heavy with child and her message sounded urgent, she would have to wait just a little longer.

"Och, my lady, I didna even see ye standin' there."

Annalyse's eyes dropped from the kissing bough to see a Scot with a tankard in his hand heading in her direction. His broad chest was large and foreboding, while his hair boasted the color of the fiery hot flames of hell. Not that she'd know what the flames of hell looked like, since she'd been raised by nuns and attended church several times a day. If the nuns hadn't been superstitious, they would have accepted her into the Order. But they didn't want The Almighty scowling down at them for bringing a cursed second-born twin into their Order and so she remained an outcast even in the eyes of God.

The Scot's craggy brows lifted and she saw a playful twinkle in his dangerous green eyes. Scots were to be feared and this one looked to be an abundance of trouble. He smiled at her. That told her he didn't know who she was or he'd be keeping his distance. With a saffron leine half-open she could see the hairs on his chest peeking out from between the leather laces of his tunic. A dark green plaid wrapped around his waist and was thrown over one shoulder and pinned with a metal badge.

She didn't dare even to breathe. Never had she ever been so close to one of these savages before and wondered if she were in danger. After all, the Scots were enemies of the English. What could this man possibly be doing in her father's castle? Her gaze shot around the room as she desperately scanned the area, looking for her sister. Gabrielle was nowhere to be seen, only ladies and knights standing under more kissing boughs. The women giggled and the men pulled them into their arms and kissed them in front of everyone. This wasn't what she expected to find at all and it would do naught to help her out of this awkward position.

"I suppose ye're waitin' for a kiss as well, my lady. Well, I willna disappoint ye."

Before she had a chance to object, the Scotsman pulled her up against his chest with one hand while he cradled his drink in the other.

"I – I think you –" She never had a chance to finish her sentence because his mouth covered hers with a big, wet kiss.

It took her by surprise and she hadn't even a moment to prepare for her first – and possibly only, kiss. It all happened so quickly that it took her breath away. She'd just been kissed by a total stranger and, surprisingly, she found that she liked it. It was exciting and intimate, and she could taste the burn of the whisky he'd been drinking as she ran her tongue over her lips.

"You didn't even give me time to object," she told him, wanting to sound like a respectable lady even if she had secretly been hoping for this to happen.

"Welcome, my lady," said the Scot, taking her by the arm and escorting her into the great hall. "I'm sure ye've heard that to reject a kiss under the kissin' bough will mean ye willna marry this year, so it is a guid thing ye didna object."

"I'm sure I won't marry this year or any year, so what does it matter?" She looked away and brushed invisible lint from her sleeve as they headed across the vast room.

"Dinna be so sure. Now that ye've had a kiss under the kissin' bough, things will change."

"I wouldn't bet on that." While the room held warmth

from the hearth and happiness in the lively decorated surroundings, she wasn't greeted with a warm welcome from the people. The music from the gallery overhead stopped and the lull of voices quieted as all eyes focused on her.

"It's the cursed one," she heard a woman whisper. Then a few other muffled voices called her a demon and spawn of the devil. A searing heat rose within her. She held mixed emotions of wanting to shout out and run to wanting to sink into the shadows and hide all at the same time.

"Annalyse?" came a soft voice from behind her. She turned to see her twin sister heading across the room, being followed by their loving mother. Identical in every way, Annalyse and Gabrielle were tall with long, blond hair that fell halfway down their backs. Annalyse's body was slim and lanky, but she had the right curves to prove to any man that she was not a girl but a woman. Gabrielle, on the other hand, had other curves. Her huge belly jutted out beneath her gown, proving to all she was the king's pregnant mistress, and about to be an unwed mother. That alone should be enough to cause tongues to wag but, instead, the gossip would revolve around her now that she had arrived in Hetherpool.

Lady Ernestine, their mother, was a petite woman. There was no mistaking the girls had inherited their height from their father.

"Daughter, I'm so happy to see you." Ernestine stepped forward and embraced Annalyse in a hug.

"Sister," said Gabrielle, giving Annalyse a hug as well, but not being able to get as near because of her protruding belly. "I'm so glad you came to join us." Gabrielle rubbed her bulge and her face said she was happy, but her eyes did not. Trouble darkened her blue orbs and Annalyse felt her sister's pain in her own heart. Something was wrong.

"Well, I'm not glad you are here," came the stern voice of her father, Lord Ramsay Granville, as he rushed across the hall with several of his knights trailing behind him. "Your presence at the castle will only cause me trouble." His eyes darted back and forth, watching the reactions of the others. "You must leave anon."

"And a warm welcome to you, too, Father," Annalyse answered with a stiff upper lip. She would not be thrown out into the cold on Christmas Eve, no matter what her father ordered. "I will not leave as I am here as an invited guest."

"A guest?" The man frowned, which made his peppered-grey mustache turn down at the ends. "I didn't invite you."

"Nay, but I did," said Gabrielle, boldly reaching out and putting her arm around Annalyse. "I am about to give birth to the king's bastard. And since I am not welcome at the king's court right now, I would like to be surrounded by the people who care about me."

"Not so loud," said her father, dismissing his knights and pulling the girls to the side. The Scotsman followed. "Musicians, play something cheery and everyone celebrate as you were," he ordered. The music started back up and though the occupants did as instructed and started dancing, their attention remained on Annalyse. "Daughter, you cannot stay. I'll be cursed if you do," said her father.

"Now, now, what kind of talk is that about yer own bairn?" asked the Scot, pushing his way in between them.

"It's true," said Lord Ramsay. "Annalyse, you know as well as I that your presence here will be considered naught but trouble. And when something bad happens, I'll be blamed for it. Now go back to the abbey where you belong." He reached around the Scot and took her arm, intending to drag her to the door, but she yanked out of his grip.

"Nay. It is Christmas, Father, and Gabrielle sent for me. I'll not spend another holiday without my family and locked away in a nunnery where I surely don't belong. Besides – you've got a cursed Highlander here, so why should it matter if I stay? He's sure to be more trouble than me."

"Lowlander," the Scot corrected her, mumbling into his tankard as he raised it to his mouth.

"Don't send her away," begged her mother.

"The Scot is Ross of Clan Douglas and has been sent by the king himself, so he belongs here. You do not," snapped her father.

"Aye, that's right. The king sent me," said the Scot with a nod of his head, raising the tankard once again.

"Why would you welcome this savage into your castle

walls while you reject your own daughter?" she cried. "I am of your blood, but he is a Douglas! Father, are you insane to invite a Douglas into your home?"

The Scot's green eyes met hers over the rim of the tankard and he squinted as he slowly lowered the drinking vessel. "I am a respectable, honored man from Clan Douglas. Perhaps ye dinna ken of the revered and noble leaders that were from our clan such as Sir William the Bold and the Black Douglas. I assure ye, I may be a lot of things but I am no' a savage," he told her, sounding insulted that she had referred to him as such. "If I were, I hardly think yer king would send me here to make an alliance."

"An alliance?" she asked in surprise, not understanding any of this. "Father, tell me this isn't true!"

"It is," her father murmured, his eyes traveling to Gabrielle's big belly. "It's not bad enough that your sister was a mistress of our king, but she now carries a bastard and is unwed. But there is a solution that will remedy that quickly."

"Annalyse," said Gabrielle, taking her hand. She felt her sister's warmth and care, but wasn't sure why a whore of the king would be accepted by all, but not her – a mere second-born twin who'd been raised by nuns. "King Edward has rejected me and no longer wants me as his mistress," her sister explained.

"Nay!" she spat, horrified that her sister had gone from being in the king's favor to being discarded so easily. "What of the king's bastard child?" asked

Annalyse. "What will become of him?"

"King Edward has rejected the babe as well," Gabrielle said, running a hand over her extended midsection. "I honestly thought he would come for his bastard as soon as it was born, but the missive he sent said just the opposite."

"This is terrible," Annalyse murmured, knowing a soiled lady would never be accepted by any noble. Now Gabrielle would be unwanted, just like her.

"Your father did the only thing he could," explained her mother with tears in her eyes. "Ross has not judged us like the English nobles."

"He hasn't?" Her eyes snapped up to interlock with the Scot's. She couldn't stop thinking about his kiss and wanted to experience it again. "What are you saying?"

"What yer mathair is tryin' to say, my lady," said the Scot with a nod of his head toward her sister. "Is that I'm betrothed to yer sister, Lady Gabrielle."

"You are?" Her heart thumped in her chest and she felt as if, once again, being the second-born twin was working against her. Her sister, once mistress to the king himself, was now discarded and pregnant yet she wouldn't be ostracized and rejected the way Annalyse had been for the last twenty years. Nay, now her lucky sister would be wife to a Lowland Scot and Annalyse would go back to the abbey alone, once again to live her life as naught more than an unwanted recluse.

Chapter 3

Ross surveyed the girls standing in front of him with interest. The two sisters looked so much alike that it was uncanny. Twins, he'd been told. Aye, they obviously were. Both had long blond tresses twisted into braids that trailed down their backs. And both had bright blue eyes that reminded him of a bird - intense and always watching. So clear and bright were their eyes that the fact alone made them unique from the rest of the lassies he'd seen. Not to mention they were both bonnie and a pleasure to gaze upon.

The girls were tall, but the pregnant one seemed meek. The one that looked like a nun was far from meek and had a fire about her that excited him. He'd enjoyed the kiss and wondered if the girl's sister that he was to marry kissed with such passion, as well.

Chuckling inwardly, he thought how alike yet different they were at the same time. One lassie was soiled and huge with a bairn, while the other looked to be pious the way she was covered up like a nun. He knew neither of them, but the kiss he'd shared with the cursed twin seemed like a blessing to him. Her lips were soft and sweet, and he'd tasted her innocence intermingling with a dormant spark of wild passion. Coming across as timid and reserved at first, he'd seen something entirely different when he'd gazed into her eyes. He'd seen a restless soul that needed to be released. Although he was already betrothed to her sister, he wanted to be the one to release the pent-up passion in the holy one.

"Lady Gabrielle, as yer betrothed, I'd like to have this dance with ye." He gave his tankard to a serving boy and extended his hand to the pregnant twin. His plan with the faked alliance and betrothal was working perfectly, so far. The dowry the girl's father was providing was more than substantial. Now his clan would be aligned with an English border lord as well, with the best part being that he would now be taking from the English king, instead of the king taking from him.

"Oh, no, I couldn't dance," Gabrielle said, pulling her hand back and rubbing her belly. He'd never seen a woman so huge during her pregnancy and realized it might be better if she just sat down, instead. The king's baby was sure to be a giant and the Scots could always use another good-sized, strong warrior. Hopefully, he could move his plan along quickly, before the king found out what he'd done. If not, everything would be ruined. "Annalyse, please dance with Ross in my stead."

"Me?" Annalyse's eyes opened wide. Ross didn't miss the way the frightened girl's gaze darted over to her father. "I don't think I'd better."

"Nonsense," said her mother, stepping forward, and guiding Annalyse toward him. "I want you to stay and celebrate Christmas with us. It has been too long and I miss you."

"So do I," chimed in Gabrielle.

"She's not staying," growled her father. "Or didn't you hear me?"

"Lord Ramsay, if ye'd allow me to have just one dance with yer daughter, I'd be ever so grateful," Ross said, eying the roomful of occupants who seemed to snub the girl. "I ken exactly how she must feel since it is no secret that most of the Englishmen here reject me, as well."

"That will soon change for you since we now have an alliance between us," snorted Lord Ramsay. The lord had not been happy when he'd read the king's missive. Ross and his men entered into the castle's walls just after the messenger left. It had worked to his advantage and no one was the wiser. The king's seal was intact. The words on the parchment had not been questioned by anyone.

"Then mayhap if they see me dancin' with the cursed twin, they'll accept no' just one – but both of yer daughters."

"I don't think that's a good idea."

"Please, my lord," begged Lady Ernestine, the man's wife. "Let her stay. It'll be good to have another woman present at the birth of your grandchild."

"Grandchild? Ha!" said the lord. "I'll never see my grandchild since the king plans on sending both my daughter and her baby across the border. Besides, we have a midwife and servants to help with the birth, so Annalyse is not needed."

"Father, I want Annalyse by my side," said Gabrielle. "I'm frightened and she knows what I'm feeling more than anyone since we often feel the same things."

"Hush," said her father. "Talk like that will only roil the crowd."

"Please, Father, it is Christmastime," begged Annalyse. "Besides, I'd like to stay and let the others see that it is naught but superstition that I am cursed. I want to prove to them that I will not bring bad luck upon the occupants of this castle."

"I agree," said Gabrielle. "Let her stay at least through the holidays and until I've birthed my baby."

"Yer daughter could be an asset at a time like this," said Ross. "With her here, it'll free up more time for us to talk about another possible alliance between the Scots and English in the near future."

Ramsay laughed. "Hah! If you're suggesting any Scot would be addled enough to want to marry a cursed second-born twin, then mayhap we should talk after all."

"I dinna see anything wrong with the lassie," said Ross, managing to make the girl's face turn a shade of bright red.

"Then by all means dance with her and I'll give my knights another round of drinks to distract them." The lord of the castle headed away through the crowd.

"My lady?" Ross held his hand out to the girl, but she was hesitant in accepting his offer.

Annalyse stood petrified, not sure what to do. She should feel elated that her father decided to let her stay through the birth of her sister's baby, but something about the whole situation didn't feel right. This man was her sister's betrothed and after the kiss they'd shared, she'd started fantasizing what it would be like if she were the one to be marrying the Scot, instead. Her upbringing in the convent made her feel ashamed of such a thought, but her rebellious side made her want to not only dance with the Scot but kiss him under the kissing bough again.

"I – I'm not sure," she said, looking over to her sister. "Gabrielle, I came here to help you and I can see you are very uncomfortable."

"I just need to sit down," said Gabrielle. "In my condition, I can't dance. I don't want to disappoint my betrothed, so please go in my place."

"Yes, I agree. Don't worry; I will stay with Gabrielle," said her mother. "Please dance with the Scot so the others won't be suspicious of you, Annalyse." Her mother smiled and ran a hand over Annalyse's arm. "I'm happy you have returned to Hetherpool. I'm hoping your father will see that it is naught but superstition that you are ill luck and that he will let you stay here instead of going back to the nunnery."

"Really?" Annalyse felt a knot forming in her throat and was too choked up to speak. Perhaps, once Gabrielle was married to the Scot and moved away over the border, Annalyse could take her place. She hated living in the abbey and had only wanted to live in the castle like she should have instead of being sent away in the first place. "All right, I'll do it for you, Gabrielle."

Annalyse hesitantly reached out, placing her hand on the Scot's arm. He covered her hand with his as they walked and it was so large she felt as if she were being devoured.

"I feel how tense ye are, m'lady," he told her. "Dinna worry about a thing. Ye're with me now and I'll protect ye from the daggered looks ye're gettin' from the crowd."

"Thank you," she said, not sure if his offer of protection made her feel more secure or more uncomfortable since he'd pointed out everyone was staring at her. "I'm not that sure about the dance, as we don't partake in this activity at the abbey."

"Then I'll lead ye, and ye just follow," he said, flashing her a smile of strong, straight, white teeth. He was ever so handsome. Taking her into his arms, he guided her through the steps of the dance and, after a few minutes, she found that she'd remembered the actions after all. "Ye are a fast learner." He leaned up against her body and his warmth made her tingle with anticipation. It felt good to be so close to a man. The Scots must dance closer than the English, who usually left space between them.

"I suppose I remember the dance from childhood after all," she told him, not able to look him in the eye for fear he'd see her desire to kiss him again.

"How long have ye been a nun?"

"Oh, I'm not a nun!" She almost shouted her words as

she denied the accusation. "I've only been raised by nuns; that's all."

"Really? That's interestin'." He twirled her around and she dared to glance up at his handsome face once more. Gabrielle was far too lucky to be getting a man like Ross. She despised her sister for a mere moment, wishing she were the one marrying the Scot. "I've never heard of anyone bein' raised in a convent and no' joinin' the Order," he continued.

"It seems nuns are superstitious as well." She faced him and curtsied as he bowed and they continued the dance as he led her across the floor with his chin raised as if he were proud of accompanying her. For the first time in her life, she felt like a noblewoman. The feeling made her heady and she found it hard to breathe. "They didn't want the wrath of God on their heads for bringing a spawn of the devil into the Order," she told him under her breath.

He laughed and the deep timbre of his voice resounded through the room. It felt good to make a man laugh, even if he was laughing at her misfortune.

"I dinna believe in superstitions and I think it is a guid thing ye are no' a nun."

She stopped the dance as the music ended and looked up into his mesmerizing green eyes. "What do you mean?"

"What I mean, lassie, is that by the way ye kiss, I am sure, someday, ye will make a guid wife to a verra lucky man."

"No man will ever want me." Bile rose in her throat

and she felt as if she wanted to retch. The truth was sickening and she wished to go back to the feeling she'd had when he'd proudly displayed her on the dance floor. That had made her feel like a noblewoman. But now she felt more like a leper, thinking of having to grow old all alone just because she was born the second twin.

"If I wasna already betrothed to yer sister, I would scoop ye up before another man could."

"You – you would?" She wasn't sure if he was saying this as a jest or with sincerity, as he was very hard to read.

He didn't have a chance to answer because her father came over and interrupted them.

"Ross, I'd like you to join me and some of my knights at the hearth for a drink."

"Aye," he said with a nod of his head. "I'd like a dram of whisky."

They left and Annalyse suddenly felt insecure and all alone. She spotted her sister on the bench at the dais along with her mother and walked over to join them.

"Annalyse, stay with your sister while I find the chambermaid and make certain she prepares a room for you during your visit," said her mother.

"Thank you, Mother." She sat down on the bench next to her sister. Immediately feeling her sister's fear, she reached out and touched her hand. "I feel that you're frightened, Gabrielle, but you don't have to worry. I'm here to help you through this birth. Women give birth every day and this will be no different."

"I feel things as well, Sister, and what I feel is your

attraction to the Scot," said Gabrielle with a slight smile.

"Surely, I don't know what you mean." Annalyse pulled her hand away from her sister, not wanting any more of her secrets revealed.

"He is a very handsome man and I cannot blame you for having eyes for him," said Gabrielle. "But I am to marry him and, sadly, he is not my king." The smile left her face and she shook her head. "You would be better suited for the Scot than I."

"We both know that can never happen." Annalyse's heart dropped to her stomach knowing she would probably never get the opportunity to marry in this lifetime. "If I had been born first, mayhap things would be different."

She felt Gabrielle's uncomfortable reaction to that statement. If her sister hadn't been so heavy with child, Annalyse might have thought there was another reason for the way she stirred restlessly on the chair.

"Annalyse, I need to talk to you." Tears formed in Gabrielle's eyes.

"You're upset," answered Annalyse knowingly. "Is it because the king has rejected you and your baby?"

"Nay," she said, using the square linen cloth on the table to wipe her eyes. "It's more than just that. I am terrified of this birth and am afraid it will end up being horrible and cursed in the end."

Annalyse quickly stood and put her hands on her hips. "If you're thinking I'm going to curse the birth of your baby, why did you send for me in the first place?"

"Nay, Sister, this has naught to do with you." Gabrielle reached out and took Annalyse's hand in hers.

"What do you mean?"

"Feel for yourself and I think you'll understand." Gabrielle placed Annalyse's palm on her belly and took a deep breath and released it slowly.

Annalyse was about to ask her again what she meant when she felt the baby kick. "He kicked," she said excitedly, smiling from ear to ear. But then she felt more kicking and still more, and she knew something was wrong. A vision flashed through her mind and suddenly she knew why her sister feared this birth. She pulled her hand back as if she'd been burned and her eyes interlocked with her sister's. On shaky legs, she sat back down. Gabrielle's eyes were filled with tears and Annalyse felt fear – not for herself but for what was about to happen.

"Gabrielle, I see why you sent for me now. And you are right – this birth will be horrible and cursed."

"So you felt it, too?" asked her sister.

"I did," said Annalyse, shaking her head and leaning closer to whisper so no one would hear them. "This is not good, Sister. I think you are about to birth the king not one . . . but two bastards!"

Chapter 4

"Two babies at the same time?" Tears fell from Gabrielle's eyes. She shook her head furiously as if she thought that action could shake away the horrible situation she was in. "They'll be feared and cursed – and I'll die giving birth!"

"Nonsense," said Annalyse putting her arm around her sister's shoulder to calm her, though she agreed with her completely. She didn't wish on any baby the lifestyle with which she'd been inflicted. "Mother birthed us and did not die. Everything will be all right." Lying wasn't a good thing to do when your twin sister could read your thoughts and feelings.

"You fear for the babies and me as well," said Gabrielle. "I know it."

"All right, I do," she finally admitted, no longer able to keep it inside. She noticed the Scot look up from the other side of the room. "Keep your voice down or someone will hear you. We'll just have to keep this secret to ourselves."

"You're addled if you think we can keep this a secret," said Gabrielle, crying even more. "And when Edward finds out, he'll use it against Father. This is awful."

"You don't need to tell me, I know." Feeling an edge of resentment toward her sister, an evil part of her felt satisfied that now Gabrielle would know how it felt to be called cursed. "I've lived as the cursed twin for the last twenty years while you had everything I always wanted. Mayhap, now you'll know how I felt after all."

"How can you say that, Sister? I felt your pain every day. I begged Father to bring you back from the abbey, and when he wouldn't, I went to the king to see if he could help."

"You did?" Annalyse had never known this before now.

"I managed to secure the position of the queen's lady-in-waiting and knew I could use that as an advantage to talk to the king about you."

"What did he say?"

Gabrielle dabbed at her eyes, bit her lip, and looked down to her belly. "I never had a chance to ask. Before I knew it, he'd taken me as his mistress and then I became too frightened to ask him about you."

"So the king doesn't know you have a twin sister?"

Gabrielle shook her head. "Father told the king he had no male heir and that I was his only child. I couldn't make him look bad in the king's eyes."

Annalyse jumped up from her chair and put her hands on her hips in frustration. "You say you tried to help me, but you didn't! You only thought about yourself. Well, you deserve everything you got and now I'm sorry I came here at all." Hurrying across the great hall, she quickly slipped out the door and into the night. Running across the courtyard with her cloak billowing out behind her, she didn't stop until she reached the mews. She rushed inside and threw herself down in the hay, crying, realizing not even her twin had her best interests in mind. Loneliness swelled in her chest and she couldn't help but feel sorry for herself. No one cared about her and no one would miss her should she leave this earth forever. At times like this, she wished she had never been born at all.

She wasn't sure how long she lay there crying, but after some time she had the feeling that she wasn't alone. Someone was in the mews besides the birds; she felt it deep inside.

"Who's there?" she called out, looking around the darkened mews with wide eyes. "Make yourself known or I'll cut you to pieces." She pulled up the edge of her gown and grabbed for the dagger strapped to her leg. Nuns didn't carry weapons and she'd kept this her secret since she knew she couldn't count on anyone to protect her. Standing up, she made her way to the rail, scoping the area, listening intently since she was sure she'd heard footsteps. From behind her, a falcon squawked and fluttered its wings, scaring her and causing her to jump.

Her body spun around in a half-circle and her arms shot forward, holding her dagger with both hands as it wavered in the air. "I'll stab you. I swear I will. Now, make your presence known." A shiver ran down her spine and her legs quaked beneath her as her thoughts ran rampant. Had an angered inhabitant or two come to kill the cursed daughter of the lord of the castle before misfortune fell upon their heads?

Someone touched her shoulder and she cried out. Annalyse twirled around, waving her dagger wildly through the air.

"Losh me, stop that!" Ross' hand shot out and grabbed her wrist, stilling her action. "If ye keep that up, ye're goin' to hurt someone, lassie."

"That's the idea!" She still didn't let down her guard. "I have to fend for myself since I'm all alone. No one wants to help me – they just want to hurt me."

"No' me, lassie. I came to see if ye're all right. I saw ye leave the hall cryin' and yer sister is cryin', too."

"I'm not crying," she said looking the other way. He took the dagger from her, shoving it under his belt and she crossed her arms over her chest.

"Want to tell me what it is that made no' one, but two lassies cry?"

"Nay. It's none of your concern. Now, leave me be." She looked the other way to avoid getting trapped into telling him the truth.

He stepped in front of her. "It is my concern if I'm goin' to marry into yer family." He reached out his hand and brushed a tear away from her eyes with his thumb.

"Why are you so kind to me when everyone else shuns me?" she asked.

"Mayhap that's why. I dinna need to remind ye that I am a Scot. We're no' loved or accepted by the English, but yer faither has made an alliance with me by betrothin' me to yer sister."

"Then go to her and leave me be."

"I canna, lassie. Ever since our kiss, I canna think of anyone else but ye."

"You – you liked the kiss?" Slowly, her arms dropped to her sides and she looked directly at him. Even in the dark, she could see the sincerity in his eyes. There was an attraction between them; there could be no denying. His long red hair hung down as he leaned in closer to her. A straight nose and chiseled cheekbones made him look so handsome that for a mere moment, all her troubles faded away. His short red beard and mustache made him seem distinguished as he kept his eyes focused on her mouth.

"Ye tell me," he said, leaning over further and kissing her again. Their lips melded together and his arms closed around her, pulling her up against his broad chest. Her head tilted backward and she let him kiss her, not being exactly sure why she wasn't pushing him away. He was her sister's betrothed, but Annalyse no longer cared. Some wickedness deep within her wanted Gabrielle to know that she had been kissing her man. She hated the fact Gabrielle had everything in life and she had nothing. This would be her justice for everyone and everything that had ever wronged her. Or so she thought. What started as a vengeful game turned into something else quickly, scaring her when she realized she couldn't stop herself. Reaching up and putting her hands on his shoulders, she pulled the Scot even closer and deepened the kiss, getting caught up in the intimate moment. Then to her surprise, his tongue shot out into her mouth, exciting her even more. She wanted to try this, too. Her sister had known the ways of coupling with a man, but she'd been denied the same opportunity. At twenty years of age, Annalyse was well past marrying age and also tired of being pushed off and considered a nun. This time, she would feel what her sister had felt all the times she'd kissed a man and nothing was going to stop her from experiencing it.

"Kiss me again," she said. Before he could answer, she reached up and kissed him, letting her tongue enter his mouth this time, getting a moan in return from the Scot. Then his hands started to roam and she felt him squeeze her rump as he pulled her against his hardened form. Suddenly seeing where this was leading, she realized her game had gone too far. If she wasn't careful, the Scot might throw her down in the hay and have his way with her right here. Annalyse's pious upbringing reared its head and shame filled her senses for what she'd just done with another woman's betrothed. Pushing away from him, she wiped her mouth with the back of her hand.

"Don't try that again or next time I really will stab you." Her hand shot out and she yanked her dagger from his waist belt, causing him to jump back in surprise. The birds became startled, watching and listening from their perches. The smell of hay and lust filled the air, and while she felt ashamed and held back her tears, he only chuckled.

"I think I'm marryin' the wrong twin," he said with a devious grin. "I like a woman with fire in her veins."

"Well, I'm not your betrothed and I warn you not to try anything with me again or I'll tell my sister."

That only made him laugh harder. "I wouldna suggest that, unless ye want me to reveal to her the way ye were kissin' me. That, my lady, was no' the kiss of a lassie who didna enjoy it."

"Darn, that kissing bough," she spat, blaming this whole thing on the fact she'd been lingering under the mistletoe when she'd first arrived, secretly hoping to experience a kiss. And now that she had, she found herself only wanting more. She was a cursed twin and didn't deserve this, she reminded herself silently. She could never have this. This man wasn't hers – he was her sister's. No matter what happened, it seemed her sister always won and she lost. Yes, Annalyse was certain she would continue to live her life doomed by the hand of God alone.

Chapter 5

The next day was Christmas and, although Annalyse told herself she would leave the castle and go back to the nunnery, she found herself staying, instead. Her sister thought she was staying to help her through the birth, but Annalyse wasn't sure if that was her reason or if it was just because she wanted to see Ross again.

Standing behind the partition leading to the kitchen, she watched as her family sat at the dais table eating their Christmas meal. She'd overslept and no one had come to wake her, so the meal had started without her. She wasn't sure if she was welcome at the dais but guessed not since no one had come to call for her. Her sister had lent her one of her gowns and she felt noble for the first time in her life, but not confident enough to march up to the dais and sit down with her family.

Her father sat at the center of the long trestle table with her mother at his right side. Gabrielle sat next to her and Ross sat next to her father. The Scot looked up and saw her standing there, so she quickly ducked behind the screen, almost knocking into a serving girl in the process.

"I'm sorry," she said, but the girl wouldn't even look at her. Instead, the girl blessed herself and hurried away.

All the other servants coming from the kitchen made a wide circle, walking around her, careful to avoid accidentally touching her. She was about to go back to her chamber when Ross stepped around the wall, his big body blocking her path.

"Lady Annalyse," he said. "I was wonderin' where ye were. Why are ye lurkin' around back here instead of sittin' at the dais like yer sister?"

"I'm not sure I'm welcome at my father's table," she told him.

"Why no'?" he asked. "Yer sister is heavy with a bairn and has no husband and yet she sups with yer faither. Come, join us at the table." He held out his hand and she considered taking it, but then thought how angry her father would be and just shook her head.

"Nay, I can't. I'll get something to eat from the kitchen and take it back to my chamber."

"Nay, ye'll come with me and sit at the dais. That's where the nobles eat. I'll no' let ye sit alone in yer chamber, nor will I let ye sit with the servants below the salt." He took her arm and started walking, and she had no choice but to go with him.

Once again, when she entered the great hall, all talking ceased and the room became quiet. She tried to ignore all the onlookers gawking at her and whispering behind their hands. She wanted to be here, but at the same time, she didn't want to become a spectacle. Why couldn't the servants bow and curtsy to her the way they did for her sister? If only she had been born first, things would be so different.

"Annalyse, what are you doing here?" growled her father as Ross marched her in front of the dais table.

"I'm hungry," she told him and left it at that.

"I'll have a servant bring food to you in your chamber." Her father started to raise his hand to call one over, but Ross stopped him.

"Please, my lord, if ye dinna mind, I'd like Annalyse to join us at the dais."

"Nay, it's not a good idea," said Ramsay, looking around the room nervously. "People might start to talk."

"They're already talking, Father." She spoke up bravely because Ross' actions made her want to defend herself. "And it's not just about me, but Gabrielle as well if you haven't noticed."

"It's Christmas," said her mother. "Please, let her stay."

"Yes, Father. I'd like her to stay as well," said Gabrielle putting on one of her sweetest smiles. It was getting harder to read her sister's thoughts now that the twin bastards in her womb seemed to interfere with her ability to share her sister's feelings.

"Sit down then and try not to cause trouble," growled her father, finally giving in. He picked up his goblet and chugged down a cupful of wine.

Ross seated Annalyse next to him, holding the chair for her. No one had ever done this for her before. She liked the feeling and tried to block out the staring sea of eyes watching her from below the salt.

"Ye'll share a trencher with me," said the Scot, picking up a platter from the table that held the best cuts of venison upon it. He used his eating knife to stab a piece of meat and put it on the trencher, the old stale bread they used as a plate.

"Oh my!" she said as a servant laid a platter before them with an entire swan gracing the dish. The bird had been cooked, re-feathered, and placed back on the platter to look as if it were not dead at all. This was followed by several courses of root vegetables and frumenty – a thick Christmas porridge of boiled wheat mixed with currants, yolks of eggs, and exotic spices.

Along with the food, Ross made sure to keep the drinking vessel they shared filled with spiced mead. Annalyse ate and drank her fill, feeling so full she thought she would burst. Being used to the plain, simple food in the nunnery, she'd almost forgotten about the delicacies enjoyed by the nobles.

"Now, here is a piece of mince pie for ye, my lady," said Ross, slipping a piece onto the trencher.

"Oh, no, I am so full I couldn't eat a bite." She shook her head and held up a hand, signaling that she had eaten more than enough.

"Sister, you mustn't refuse mince pie on Christmas or you will have bad luck," Gabrielle reminded her from the other end of the table.

"Lord knows I don't need any more bad luck," she said, looking down to the shredded spiced meat and fruit that filled the crust of the pie. It did look delicious.

Mayhap she could just take one bite to ensure good luck. It was only a superstition, but she didn't need anyone blaming her for bad luck if she didn't at least taste the pie.

"Make a wish with your first bite. Whatever you wish will come true," said her mother, reminding her of the tradition.

Annalyse paused and looked over to her sister, thinking of all the years Gabrielle had everything that she should have had as well. Then she looked at her father scowling at her and realized this might be the last time she ever ate at the dais with her family. If Ross hadn't been here, she'd be eating by herself in her chamber right now. Feeling thankful to the Scot, and since this would never happen again, she decided to enjoy it.

"Go ahead, make a wish," said Ross, picking up some mince pie on the spoon and holding it up to her mouth. He looked so brave and handsome and seemed to be the only one who cared about her. Why couldn't she be the one marrying him? She didn't understand why the Scot would even want Gabrielle since she was the king's cast-off and very pregnant.

"Aye, I know exactly what I'll wish for," she said, closing her eyes, letting Ross guide the mince pie into her mouth. When the burst of flavor filled her senses, she boldly wished Ross were her husband instead of her sister's betrothed. Never had she met anyone who cared about her the way this stranger did and that was something she didn't ever want to give up. When even her own father shunned her, this man went to extremes to make her feel wanted and loved. Aye, she was becoming very fond of Ross because of his kindness. Thoughts filled her head of wanting to have babies with him and lay in his arms each night feeling safe and loved.

"Tell me yer wish," said Ross, causing her eyes to spring open. Guilt washed over her as she looked at her sister's smiling face and then back to Ross who still held the spoon from which he'd just fed her. Green eyes the color of the mountainous Highlands watched her intently. It made her want, more than anything, to tell him her wish. A part of her hoped somehow he'd want it, too. But even though she'd been tempted, she couldn't tell him. Her wish would be her secret she'd take to her grave because it was a vengeful, horrid wish against her sister and she felt so ashamed that she never wanted anyone to find out.

She swallowed the mince pie and with it went the wish for her future that could never be. "I can't tell you," she said softly, licking her lips. "If I do, it might not come true."

"Do tell," her sister urged her, but she remained quiet.

"All wishes made on Christmas with the first bite of mince pie come true," her mother reassured her.

"I hope it was a guid wish, lassie," said Ross, smiling at her and making her feel as if she were the only woman in the world. His attention to her was refreshing and addicting, and she couldn't help wanting more.

"It was a very good wish," she said, looking down to the trencher and running her finger through crumbs on the table. Then to her surprise, the Scot leaned over and whispered into her ear.

"Ye wished to kiss me again, didna ye?"

A smile lit up her face, but she kept her eyes away from his.

"Nay, that's not what I wished," she told him, hoping he'd never find out that what she wanted with him was so much more than just a kiss.

Chapter 6

Ross brushed down his horse in the stable the next day with his brother, Malcolm, and his Scottish friends at his side. He'd come to Hetherpool with only three Scots, and while they had no trouble here yet, he stil didn't feel comfortable on this side of the border. The sooner he married the girl and got back to Scotland the better.

"We need to leave for Scotland as soon as possible," said Malcolm with concern in his voice. "Kind Edward is goin' to be showin' up any day and ye, brathair, are takin' too long to secure the deal. Ye are stallin' for some reason."

"Guid. Let Edward show up," said Ross, brushing the horse harder. "Mayhap I'll kill him with my bare hands to pay him back for the loss of so many of our clan and our family."

"Ye're here to make an alliance to stop the attacks onour clan," Malcolm remided him. "Now, seal the deal and let's get back over the border before the king finds out what ye've done."

"Och, Ross, he's right," said his good friend, Breac. "Ye need to hurry up, so stop wooin' the wrong sister."

"Aye, ye are betrothed to the king's hoor, yet ye seem

to have eyes for the cursed one," said Niven. "This is goin' to get us into trouble."

"Dinna call Lady Gabrielle a hoor," said Ross. "She was Edward's mistress and probably had no choice in the matter. And dinna call Lady Annalyse cursed because she is naught but a blessin'."

"Lady Gabrielle is the lover of the English king and carries his bairn!" Breac pounded his hand against the wood of the stall. "Think of what ye're doin', Ross. When Edward finds out ye've stolen her, there will be hell to pay. Ye would be better off marryin' the pious sister. At least she's not soiled and doesna carry our enemy's bastard."

"Plus, no one would come after us if ye took her," said Niven. "They all think she is cursed and would probably be happy to see her go."

"I ken what I'm doin'," Ross said, running his hand over his horse's withers as he spoke, not at all certain anymore that he had made the right decision.

"Are ye sure?" asked his brother. "Ye are puttin' not only us but our clan and our country in danger with yer crazy plan."

"I am here to take from the king someone who means somethin' to him. Just like he did to us, Malcolm. And if I can take his bastard along with his mistress - well, then all the better."

"Then marry her and let's get back to Scotland already," complained Malcolm. "That missive we intercepted from the king said he will be here soon to collect Gabrielle and the baby. The letter we forged is sure to be discovered and when it is, our heads will end up on spikes."

"Losh me, calm down, all of ye," Ross told them, feeling his nerves rattled by his friends questioning his decision. Mayhap he shouldn't have involved them in this dangerous plan at all, but they were loyal to him and he admired them for always sticking with him. "I'm goin' to marry Lady Gabrielle now that the holiday is over and we'll leave for Scotland anon."

"I heard the lady of the castle talkin' about the Feast Day of the Holy Innocents," said Niven.

"That's right. The girl's father said yer weddin' canna take place until after then, as it is an unlucky day," Malcolm pointed out.

"When is this Feast Day of the Holy Innocents?" asked Ross.

"In two days' time," Breac answered. "But the king could show up before then and if he does, what will ye do?"

"I'll pray the king doesna show until after the feast day then." Ross kissed his horse on the nose, thinking about the kiss he'd shared with Annalyse. Perhaps his friends were right and he was marrying the wrong sister. But there was naught he could do about it now. The plan was in motion and he wouldn't rock the boat. They'd go through with it as scheduled.

"What's the matter, guid friend?" asked Niven. "Ye look so sullen."

"I dinna ken," he told them, putting down the brush on a bench. "Ever since I kissed the lassie's sister, I have to admit that I'm havin' second thoughts."

"Second thoughts?" Breac came quickly to his side. "What are ye thinkin'?"

"Aye," said Niven, coming to join them. "Ye sound as if ye're considerin' givin' up yer revenge."

"Are ye?" asked Malcolm. "It would be safer. Or are ye still goin' forward with the original plan?"

"I have no choice. We will continue with the plan," said Ross, thinking once again about Annalyse. His gut twisted into a knot and he regretted that he would have to leave her behind. She was an outcast in her own land – an outcast within her own family. Born as a noble, she should be respected and honored, but just because she'd been born the second twin, her destiny was sealed and it wasn't favorable at all. Annalyse didn't deserve this treatment and he wanted more than anything to take her away with him instead of taking her bairned sister. He had to come clean and tell Annalyse about this, but he would need to make her promise not to tell anyone his secret until he was gone. But would she agree to that? Somehow, he didn't think so. Now, he thought, mayhap, he should have taken a bite of the mince pie and made a wish of his own because this is one situation he wished he could change.

"Sit down, Gabrielle, before you fall down," scolded Annalyse as she led her sister into the bedchamber and helped her settle herself on the bed.

"I don't feel well," said Gabrielle, sweat dripping from her face. Annalyse ran over to the washstand and dipped a rag in cold water. She came back and dabbed at her sister's face.

"You'll be all right," Annalyse reassured her. "You always are."

"I'm not so sure about it this time," said Gabrielle. "I think something horrible is about to happen. I feel it in my bones. Someone is going to die." The babies kicked just then. She let out a groan and placed her hands on her enormous belly.

"You have naught to worry about." Annalyse said the words but in her heart, she didn't believe them one bit. She kept thinking of her presence here possibly being the cause of this feeling. Mayhap, Gabrielle was right. Annalyse felt something unsettling in the air, as well. Hopefully, they were both wrong and nothing bad would happen.

She put the rag back into the water and settled herself on the bed next to her sister, not able to keep the thought from her mind that someone had brought ivy into the great hall and woven it into the kissing boughs. Ivy brought indoors meant death. If Gabrielle's babies died, Annalyse realized she would be blamed for bringing bad luck to the castle in the end. No one would blame it on the ivy. "You're going to marry that handsome man named Ross and live with him in Scotland. Everything will work out fine," she said trying to put her sister's fears to rest. Even with the babies blocking her connection, she still felt more fear emanating from Gabrielle than she had in her entire life. Death loomed in the air and while she would not acknowledge that she felt it, too, neither could she deny it.

"I don't want Ross." Gabrielle scowled and waved her hand through the air.

Annalyse's head snapped upwards and a tinge of hope shot through her heart. "What do you mean?"

"I am in love with my king and he is the only man I want."

"Gabrielle! You are only a mistress. Don't forget the man is married with children of his own. And he also said he no longer wants you or the baby."

"I don't believe it," she said. "I'm sure he cares about me the way I do for him and I'm sure he wants the baby. Tell me, why would he reject his own child? Something is not right."

"Mayhap his wife found out about you."

"Queen Philippa has known about us for some time."

"She has? And she hasn't sent you home long before now?"

"We have become good friends in my time of service to her."

"How can you think you're friends?" asked Annalyse in surprise. "You are bedding her husband!"

"Queen Philippa is a wonderful woman like no other. She is kind and sweet and very forgiving. She knows her husband has a mistress and more than likely several. She also knows she can't stop him and has told me that she'd rather his mistress be someone she's fond of and that she doesn't hold it against me."

"That is shocking," said Annalyse. "I wonder why, then, the king said he no longer wanted you and sent you away?"

"He sent me home to have the baby. But when I received the missive, I was surprised to find out he no longer wanted the baby or me."

"Where is the missive?" she asked. "Can I see it?"

"It's on the table by my hairbrush." Gabrielle's eyes closed and she sank lower into the pillows. "Edward is superstitious. Although he doesn't want me or his bastard, if he finds out I've birthed twins, he'll consider that a bad omen. He'll most likely order one or possibly both of the babies killed. Oh, Sister, I am so frightened. I don't know what to do."

"Sleep now, Gabrielle, and in the morning we will think up a plan of how to hide one of the babies, so no one – not even our father, knows you've birthed twins. Because if he knows, I pity the bastard who is born second."

Annalyse picked up the missive from the table, put it in her pocket and headed out to the orchard to read it alone. Walking through the crowded courtyard, she smiled at the children playing, wishing for children of her own. Handsome knights strolled over the cobblestone with their ladies holding on to their arms and she couldn't help noticing the looks of love or possibly lust between them. If only she didn't have to go back to living with the nuns, mayhap she could convince a knight or even a guard that she was not cursed and would make a suitable wife and good mother.

The day was sunny although the cold winter breeze blew strong. Still, she wanted to be alone to read the king's missive. She made her way to the orchards, settling atop a knoll of half-dead grass under an apple tree.

Trying to hold her cloak around her to block the chill, she pulled the missive from her pocket and looked at the seal on the back. She'd seen the king's seal made with his signet ring many times while she lived at the abbey. Running her hand over the broken seal, it seemed to have excess wax along the edges. She felt as if more wax had been added to the original stamp.

She raised her knees and coddled the missive in her lap as she carefully opened it and read the words within. The missive was messy, with some words smaller than the others. More than one blob of ink littered the parchment when normally the king's scribe was meticulous, paying attention to the smallest of details. The writing almost seemed to be in two different scripts as well. This message went into detail of Edward not wanting Gabrielle or the baby. It also named Ross as the man her sister was to marry, saying her father was to make an alliance with Clan Douglas. King Edward was usually long-winded and sometimes sent more than one missive to convey everything he needed to say.

He also often sent a second missive to follow up the first one that had been delivered. Since this was the only missive, she highly expected another to arrive any day now.

"I can't believe this," she said aloud, wondering why the king would want his bastard in the hands of his enemies even if he no longer wanted Gabrielle for his mistress. Something wasn't right here; Gabrielle was correct. She read the letter several times and then saw something she hadn't before. Ye. Instead of the word *you*, one of the sentences used the word *ye*.

"Ross!" she said, knowing now the man was trying to deceive her family as well as the king. "I have to tell someone." She jumped up. In the process, the wind blew the parchment from her hands. She chased the missive through the orchard, across the courtyard, and finally to the stables. Reaching out for it, she almost caught it, but a large booted foot came down atop it, stopping her from picking it up.

"Lady Annalyse, it seems ye've lost somethin'." Ross bent over and picked up the missive and scowled. "What are ye doin' with this?"

"I – I was just reading the message the king sent my sister. Now please, give it back." She reached for it, but he moved it away.

"Why would ye want this?"

"It's important. Give it to me!"

"No' until I tell ye somethin' first."

"Whatever it is can wait. Now, please give me back the missive."

"This isna exactly from the king, Annalyse. Ye see - I

tampered with it, but it was for a guid reason."

"So it was you!"

Three Scots walked out of the stable and stopped when they saw what was going on. "Ross, what are ye tellin' her?" asked one of them.

"I canna keep deceivin' her," said Ross. "I told her the truth - that I changed the king's missive."

"Nay, brathair, ye didna!" said the Scot that looked a lot like Ross, making a face. "How could ye, ye fool?"

"Lady Annalyse, ye canna tell anyone what I did," said Ross, still holding the parchment out of her reach.

"I was right in thinking you weren't to be trusted," she snapped. "Why are you trying to deceive my family as well as the king?"

"King Edward killed Ross' family," said one of the men.

"Men, that's enough," snapped Ross. "Malcolm, take this and burn it." He handed the missive to one of the Scots.

"Nay," she protested, knowing that was her only proof that the Scots were being deceitful. "You'll not get away with this. I warn you, I'll tell my father. I'll tell everyone, even the king."

"Tell them what?" Ross cocked his head and, with a flick of his hand, dismissed his men. "Who would listen to ye or even believe ye, lassie? Ye said yerself that they think of ye as trouble and cursed. Ye dinna want to bring bad luck to yer family, do ye?"

"You cur!" she spat. "Give me back that missive." She

reached out and started pounding her fists against his chest. He caught her hands in his and scooped her up in his arms. "Put me down," she commanded as he carried her into the stable.

"That's exactly what I'm goin' to do." He plopped her down in the hay and settled himself next to her. Annalyse tried to hit him again, but he grabbed both her wrists in one of his large hands and leaned over and kissed her, causing her to forget for a moment that she was angry with him at all. "I only told ye what I did because I care for ye and didna want to lie to ye, Annalyse. I have grown fond of ye and I think ye should admit that ye feel the same way about me."

"I don't! And you'll not marry my sister if I have anything to say about it. Gabrielle loves Edward. Your horrid plan is going to ruin her life and bring strife to my family when the truth is discovered."

"Just keep my secret and leave things be. No one will get hurt."

He kissed her again and she felt herself surrendering to his manly ways. Mayhap, she should just be quiet and keep his secret as he suggested. But if she did, it would most likely bring war between the Scots and the English and she couldn't let that happen. Neither could she let him marry Gabrielle when she wanted him, and her sister only wanted Edward. None of this was right, no matter what his reason.

Shouting came from outside and they both jumped to their feet. Together, they ran to the stable door.

"Lady Annalyse, where are you? Your sister needs you," called a servant. She started to go out the door, but Ross held her arm and pulled her back to him.

"Unless ye want to be blamed for the bad luck of this castle or even a war between the English and the Scots, I suggest ye keep my secret to yerself."

"I despise you for even asking me to do such a thing! I can't just let you take my sister and the king's bastard. It isn't right." She shook loose of his hold and headed out of the stable.

"Ye can come with me to Scotland," he told her. His words stopped her in her tracks. With those words came a sense of freedom and it was very tempting.

If she was able to leave England and the abbey, mayhap she could live a better life in Scotland where no one thought of her as a curse. But if he married Gabrielle, she wouldn't be able to bear the fact he took her sister to his bed each night instead of her. Once again, her sister would be the lucky one. She would just have to watch in anguish from the shadows. She turned her head slightly and spoke to him over her shoulder.

"Why would I want to go with you? To watch you bed my sister and raise the king's bastard as your own? I'd be nothing but a handmaid. Or did you, perhaps, have in mind that I'd want to be your mistress? Let me tell you that being a mistress is something my sister would do, but I would never even consider it. So don't think I would!"

"What do ye want, Annalyse, tell me," he said, using her Christian name without her title. She liked that. It felt intimate. She also liked the way it felt to be in his arms and kissing his lips. Thoughts filled her head of the wish she'd made when she ate the mince pie. Her wish had been that he was her husband instead of Gabrielle's. She couldn't admit it to him because it didn't matter. This man had a plan to get back at the English king who had taken his family from him, and she really couldn't blame him. She knew how it felt to be without a family because hers had been taken from her long ago. While she wished she were going with him to Scotland, she selfishly wanted her sister to leave so she could get all the attention from her parents. With Gabrielle gone, mayhap her father would take her back into his home and she could regain the family she'd lost so many years ago.

"I'll never tell you what I want," she spat, hurrying away from him before he kissed her again and convinced her to change her mind.

Chapter 7

Ross hadn't slept much at all that night. He woke up in the stable the next morning to see Annalyse mounting a horse. It was early in the day and the sun was just showing its first rays on the horizon. The lassie was all alone and he knew she was up to no good.

He waited until she left and then mounted his horse, not bothering with the saddle. He stayed in the shadows and tailed her to see where she would lead him. When she took the road that led to London, he realized the only place she could be going was to see the king, and he couldn't let her do that. He waited until she stopped at a stream to water her horse and then rode up behind her.

"Ye are no' goin' to tell the king anythin', lassie."

She spun around so fast she almost fell over. Ross saw her going for her dagger strapped to her leg under her gown and dismounted quickly. He took the dagger before she could get it.

"If ye go around liftin' yer skirts and showin' yer legs, ye're goin' to be askin' for trouble."

"I'm already in trouble! You never should have told me the truth about the missive because now I need to do something to stop you."

His brother and friends had tailed her yesterday to make sure she hadn't told anyone his secret. If she had, they would have had to leave Hetherpool immediately. "I am happy ye kept my secret, lassie, but tell me - why didna ye just tell yer faither?"

"I . . . didn't want to." She looked down to the ground.

"Ye ken that he'd blame it all on you bein' the cursed one, right?" He hadn't liked having to put the idea in her head that she might be blamed for the whole thing, but he had to do something to keep her quiet.

"Yes."

His heart went out to her because he realized it was true. Now, he felt like he'd only made things worse in her life and that wasn't his intention. "Lassie, leave things as they are and dinna get involved."

"I'm already involved."

"How so?" He slowly let go of her arm. "Ye should just go back to the abbey and forget ye ever met me."

"How can I?" She looked up with tears in her eyes. "I have feelings for you, Ross, that I don't understand. I should hate you for what you're doing, but I don't, and somehow I know how you feel. I didn't tell anyone your secret because I care for you. But you have put me in a predicament because I don't want to hurt my family, either, so I need to tell someone. Don't you see, I have no other option?"

"Ye are right and I feel horrible about it." He reached out and cupped her chin in his hand. "But tell me - why do ye care for me? I need to ken."

"You're the only one who has ever been kind to me or showed me any respect when everyone else shuns me and fears me. You treated me like a lady at the Christmas table and stood up for me in front of everyone, including my father."

"As I should," he said.

"Nay, you shouldn't. You are Scottish and should hate me like everyone else does."

"I could never hate ye, Annalyse. Ye are an angel and I canna imagine that others canna see that, too." He glided his hand over her cheek in a gentle caress.

"You're just saying that because you don't want me to tell your terrible secret."

"That's no' so. And dinna think I havena had second thoughts about this whole thing because I have. Ever since I met ye, I have wondered if I am marryin' the wrong twin."

"You're marrying my sister for all the wrong reasons. By trying to get revenge on King Edward, you are going to hurt Gabrielle and her baby in return."

"I guess I wasna thinkin' of that."

"Of course you weren't. When hate and vengeance get involved, people are blinded and can't see how they are hurting others."

"Ye are hurtin', too, lassie, are ye no'?"

"Yes! Very much so. You have put me in an awful position and I don't know what to do."

"Come back to the castle with me and we can try to figure out a solution."

"If I go back with you, are you still going to marry Gabrielle?"

"I dinna ken what I'll do," he said, feeling the tension as much as she did. He took her dagger and flung it into the trunk of a tree in aggravation. "I thought I had it all worked out, but then ye came along and now I am questionin' every decision I make."

"I understand your hatred for our king and rightly so," she told him. "But think of all the people you're affecting with your decision of deception."

He nodded slowly, seeing her point, but not knowing what to do. "I'm sorry I canna give ye an answer, Annalyse, but I dinna ken what to tell ye."

"Then I can't go back to the castle with you." She stormed over and ripped her dagger from the tree, clutching it tightly in her hand.

"I can make ye come with me if I have to and yer little dagger is no' goin' to stop me."

Her eyes met his in hesitation, and finally she nodded her head. "You are right, I can't fight you," she agreed. "I'll return to my father's castle with you and stay quiet, but only for one more day. On the morrow, you will give me your decision. You can go back to Scotland alone and I will keep silent about what I know, or you can marry my sister and I will tell everyone of your deception."

"Let's go," he told her, guiding her to her horse. "I will give ye my answer on the morrow, but no matter what I decide, ye willna ever tell me what to do again!"

Elizabeth Rose

Chapter 8

Annalyse tossed and turned all night long, having dreams of Ross kissing her and making love to her and marrying her instead of her sister. It was as if he'd invaded her dreams and was trying to make her feel guilty, when instead, he was the one who should feel guilty.

A knock at her door woke her. She sat up in bed to find Gabrielle peeking inside the room.

"Get up, sleepy head," said her sister, waddling over to the window to pull the tapestry away. With it came the sunshine but also a crisp breeze.

"Oh, close it. I'm cold," complained Annalyse, burrowing down into the covers. Her hand snaked under the pillow and something pinched her. "Ow!" she said and pulled away from the pillow, holding up a sprig of greenery. "How did this get here?"

"That's mistletoe from the kissing bough," said Gabrielle, sitting down at the edge of the bed. "I put it under your pillow last night."

"Why would you do a thing like that?" Annalyse

60

yawned and stretched.

"Did you dream of a man last night?" she asked. Since Annalyse was still sleepy, she answered, not thinking of what she was saying.

"Yes! The handsome Scotsman, Ross, invaded my dreams all night long and I couldn't get rid of him."

"Ross?" Gabrielle giggled. "Oh my, that is funny."

"Why?" she asked.

"Sister, you obviously do not remember the Christmas legends. If you sleep with a sprig of mistletoe under your pillow, you will dream of the man you are going to marry."

"Marry?" That got her attention and she pushed upward on the bed. "But I can't marry Ross. He is betrothed to you!"

"Mayhap you can," she said with a smile.

"Gabrielle, what do you mean? And why do you seem so happy this morning?"

"I am happy because I received another missive today from Edward."

"Edward?" Her heart sped up. "Do you mean our king?"

"King . . . lover . . . whatever you want to call him." She played with the velvet bed curtains and kicked her feet in the air. "He's changed his mind and still wants the baby and me. He is on his way here to be with me when I give birth."

"What?" She threw off the covers and put her feet over the edge of the bed. "Are you sure?"

"Of course I'm sure. The missive said he should be here sometime today."

"Oh, Sister, I am so happy for you!" She thought of Ross and his deception, and her smile disappeared. No matter what the consequences were, she had to tell her sister. Perhaps she could somehow convince Gabrielle to keep Ross' secret as well. "Gabrielle, I have something I need to tell you."

"Whatever it is can wait until after we break the fast. These babies are hungry and I need some food." Gabrielle struggled to get off the bed and Annalyse helped her. But as soon as she got to her feet on the floor, Gabrielle doubled over in pain and water from her womb leaked down her legs.

"Oooooh, I think it's time," she moaned. A look of pain, as well as fear, spread across her face.

"Gabrielle, are the babies coming?" Annalyse hurried around the room and dressed quickly.

"Yes! Go find the midwife, please," said her sister holding on to the bedpost.

"Let me help you lie down on the bed first." Annalyse helped her sister to get comfortable while her mind told her that they had to keep these births a secret. "Gabrielle, we can't trust the midwife to keep our secret."

"Yes, we can," she said and moaned again. "She is the same midwife that birthed us. I assure you she knows how to keep a secret."

"Why do you say that? Is there a secret she's kept?"

"Just go get her," she ordered, moaning in pain. "Tell

mother, too. She will want to be here. Just be certain not to tell father until after we decide how to hide the second twin."

"I'm going," she said and hurried out the door. Making her way quickly to the great hall, she stopped at the entrance realizing nobody was in there but a few servants. Shouting and noise caught her attention from the courtyard. She quickly exited the great hall, horrified to find adults beating children with switches. The children wailed loudly and her heart went out to them.

"Stop it! Stop hitting the children," she said, racing forward. But her father intercepted.

"Annalyse, you're making a spectacle of yourself. Now hush up," he told her.

"Father, they are hitting the innocent children! Make them stop it."

"It's the Feast Day of the Holy Innocents," he reminded her. "You might not know about this since they don't do it at the abbey, but I assure you it's a tradition."

"Nay, they don't do this at the abbey and neither should anyone do it here."

"It's done to remind others of the day Herod ordered all the babies killed as he tried to find the Baby Jesus," he told her.

"Babies," she said, her heart jumping. She had almost forgotten that her sister was above stairs all alone and about to birth her babies.

"This is a bad luck day, Daughter. No one does anything of importance upon this cursed day."

"Cursed day," she repeated, wondering what her father would say when he found out his grandchildren were born on this day. He would probably blame everything on them for their entire life, not unlike what he'd done to her.

A young boy dressed as a bishop walked through the courtyard next. She remembered that it was a mock production and the boy chosen for this could do everything that a clergyman could do, except for saying mass. This event happened only on the Feast Day of the Holy Innocents.

"The mock marriages are happening now," said her father. "Where is your sister? I'd like her to marry the Scot in a mock marriage to prepare for the real one."

"Gabrielle is . . . taking a bath," she lied. "She won't be able to participate."

She saw Ross and his men gathering around the young boy who was acting as bishop for the day. Anyone participating in the mock marriage would be married for the day only. On the morrow, all would go back to normal.

"You can step in for her so the Scot can practice." Her father pushed her forward and directed her across the crowded courtyard and toward the boy bishop.

"Nay, I can't do this right now," she said. But the crowd was noisy and her father either didn't hear her or didn't care.

"Ross Douglas, you'll marry my daughter in a mock ceremony," said her father, putting her hand in the Scot's.

"My lord?" asked Ross with a raised brow.

"It's a tradition," said her father. "It'll be a mock marriage and only last a day. I'd have you marry Gabrielle, but she is bathing and will miss everything. So just use my other daughter for practice."

"Practice?" Ross looked over at her. Annalyse knew she wasn't going to get away from here until her father got what he wanted.

"Well, I did dream of him," she said to herself, figuring she may as well go along with it since this would be the closest she ever got to ever being married.

The boy said the vows. Once he pronounced them married, the crowd cheered, encouraging them to kiss.

"Nay, I can't," she said, but Ross played along. He got down on one knee and sat her atop it and looked her in the eye.

"Bonnie lassie, now that ye're my wife for the day, will ye kiss me and make this crowd stop shoutin'?"

"Fine!" she said, needing this to be over so she could go about helping her sister. She kissed him with a small peck on the mouth. When she tried to get up, he pulled her back down, covering her mouth with his and leaning her backward as he kissed her so deeply and passionately that she almost forgot what she was doing in front of a crowded courtyard.

"All right, enough," grumbled her father. "You'd think you were marrying *her* instead of my other daughter."

Annalyse stood up. Noticing the midwife across the

courtyard, she ran toward her.

"Midwife," she said, taking her by the arm. The woman turned to face her.

"Is it time?" she asked.

Annalyse nodded. "Yes, but keep it to yourself. Tell no one."

"Where is your sister?"

"She's in my chamber. Now, hurry as she is in much pain."

"Aye, my lady."

Annalyse turned around to look for her mother and bumped into Ross.

"Ooof," she said, putting out her hands, feeling his hard chest and corded muscles beneath his leine.

"Wife, where are ye goin' so fast?" he asked with a chuckle.

"I have matters to attend to, so please move out of my way." She took a step to go around him, but he blocked her path. Letting out an exasperated breath, she tried to rid herself of him once more. "I have no time for this, now please move."

"I saw the midwife rush away and I heard ye tell her to keep somethin' a secret. Is Gabrielle havin' her baby?"

"She is," Annalyse told him since she knew he wouldn't move until she gave him an answer. "But please don't tell anyone yet."

"Why no'? Is somethin' the matter?"

"I can't tell you. Now do me a favor and don't mention this to my father. I need to get back to Gabrielle.

Can you please find my mother and bring her to my chamber?"

"Of course, lassie, but tell me more."

"We will talk later," she said and hurried away, eager to get back to Gabrielle. Her sister was in pain, lots of pain, and Annalyse felt it, too. Sharing the feelings of her twin sister was exhausting at a time like this.

Finally making it back to the room, she found the old midwife leaning over the bed.

"How is she?" Annalyse asked, closing the door and walking forward.

"She is losing a lot of blood and something is very wrong," said the midwife. "She shouldn't be birthing a baby on the Feast Day of the Holy Innocents. It will bring bad luck to us all."

"Hush," she told the midwife, going to the head of the bed to comfort her sister. "Breathe," she told Gabrielle, taking her hand. Gabrielle breathed heavily and sweat dripped from her brow. The midwife prepared her for the birth and positioned herself between the girl's legs to catch the baby.

"She should be using a birthing chair but can't sit up since she is so big," said the midwife. "I've seen this before." The midwife's face went ashen and she looked over to the girls. "You know what this is, don't you?" she asked in a shaky voice.

Gabrielle was in too much pain to speak, but Annalyse nodded. "Yes, we know it is twins," she told the old woman. "And we know it'll be considered a curse if anyone finds out. You have to stay quiet about this. Gabrielle said we could trust you with the secret."

"Nay," she said shaking her head and getting off the bed. "I have lived for the last twenty years regretting the last secret I kept. I can't do it again so don't ask me to do such a thing."

"Last secret?" Annalyse didn't understand. There seemed to be something that only she didn't know. "What secret are you talking about?"

Gabrielle shouted out in pain and tears rolled down her cheeks. "Annalyse, I'm going to die. I won't go to my grave before I tell you that I am sorry for not telling you sooner. But I didn't know until we were ten and, by then, I felt it was too late." She moaned and gritted her teeth. "I couldn't go to an abbey and live like a nun; I just couldn't."

"What are you talking about?" Annalyse let go of her sister's hand.

"You are the first-born twin, not me!" Gabrielle screamed out in pain and cried harder. "I am the cursed one. And now God is punishing me for keeping the secret from you. I am birthing cursed bastards and I will die doing it. I am so sorry, Sister. I never knew how hard or how horrible it would be for you."

"I – I'm not the second-born twin?" Annalyse's heart almost stopped at this announcement. Had she heard correctly? How could someone keep a secret like this from her for her entire life? She'd gone to hell and back by being the second-born twin and now found out that it was Gabrielle who should have suffered all along. Annalyse looked over to the midwife wanting to rip off her head. "You knew, old woman, and yet you let me live in misery my entire life? Why would you do such a horrible thing?"

"Don't blame her, it was my mistake," came a woman's voice from behind her and she turned to see her mother standing in the doorway with Ross at her side. "I mixed up the babies after they were born and I thought Gabrielle was the first-born twin. You both looked identical and it was an honest mistake."

"Why didn't you tell my mother she was wrong?" Annalyse shouted at the midwife as tears flowed from her eyes. "You delivered us, so you knew the truth. Why didn't you tell her I wasn't the cursed one, but my sister was, instead?"

"I tried to, but by the time she understood what I was saying, it was too late," wailed the midwife. "Your father had already branded you as the cursed twin. When we told him, he said he would not make a fool of himself by telling everyone he'd made a mistake."

"Nay!" She shook her head not wanting to believe this was true. "We are twins, so someone could have switched us and no one would have known better. My entire family knew this shameful secret and yet you all let me live the life of a nun. I have been blamed for everything that has ever gone wrong. My entire life, others have shunned me and acted as if I had the plague. How could you do this to me, Mother? How could you condemn me to a life of hell when I didn't deserve it?"

Her mother reached for her, but she pushed the woman's hand away. Then Gabrielle called out for her, but Annalyse wanted naught to do with her sister anymore.

"You deserve to birth these twin bastards, Gabrielle," Annalyse spat in vengeance. "I will be sure that everyone knows about it now. You will feel the painful life of one of your own children, so you will know what it feels like to be the second-born twin after all." She'd been trying to help her sister, but now she wanted the girl to suffer for the secret she'd kept for the last ten years.

"You're having twins?" asked her mother sounding apprehensive. "Oh, please tell me this isn't so."

"It is," said Annalyse. "And Gabrielle deserves it. Although I feel sorry for the cursed child, my sister will finally know what it feels like to have one of her children rejected by everyone, especially her own family." She shot across the room meaning to leave, but Ross caught her in his arms and held her there, closing the door.

"Let me go," she cried, pounding her fists against his chest.

"Ye're my wife for the day and ye'll stay here with yer sister because I command it."

"I'm not your wife," she said. "You're betrothed to Gabrielle, a cursed woman now. So how does that feel?"

"Settle down, lassie, and dinna say words ye'll later regret."

Her mother gasped and before she had a chance to

respond, her sister shouted out her pain and the midwife delivered the first baby. Her mother hurried over to comfort Gabrielle while Ross pushed Annalyse forward to watch the birth.

"Those are yer nephews or nieces and ye'll no' leave before they're born," he told her.

"I need help," said the midwife. "Someone take this little boy, as there's another one coming."

"Give him to me," said her mother, taking the baby that the midwife had cut free, cleaning him with a wet rag. Annalyse stretched her neck and peeked up to see a boy with a full head of blond hair. He started crying. Suddenly, she felt horrible for the way she acted. As angry as she was, her sister needed her and so did the babies. Even if they'd deserted her in her time of need, she didn't have it in her heart to do the same in return and felt thankful that Ross had kept her from leaving.

"He's got blond hair. Like us," Annalyse told her sister, her heart softening as she drank in the miracle of birth and the helpless little child.

Her sister shouted and gritted her teeth, not able to even look at her newborn since she was in so much pain. Annalyse felt a stabbing sensation in her heart and wasn't sure if she was feeling Gabrielle's pain or pain of her own this time. Since her mother held the baby, Annalyse ran to Gabrielle's side and took her hand. Even if she despised her sister at the moment, she couldn't leave her at a time like this. Annalyse felt stabs to her abdomen next and doubled over, feeling as if she were birthing the babes herself. "Push, Gabrielle, push," she urged her sister, willing this all to be over. "Once more and then you will be done."

"They're big babies. Much too big to be twins," said the midwife. "They're tearing her apart."

Gabrielle screamed again and gripped tightly to Annalyse's hand. "I'm going to die," she cried out. Annalyse tried to stay strong, even though she saw the amount of blood covering the bed and almost screamed out.

"No, you're not going to die, Gabrielle. You're birthing the king's babies. Now just think about Edward and you'll get through this pain."

One more push and one more scream and another baby popped out.

"It's another boy," said Annalyse, looking at the baby with a smile as the midwife wiped him off. "I'm not sure how this happened, but this one has a full head of black hair."

"It's over now, Gabrielle, you can rest," said her mother, as the midwife cut the cord on the second baby.

"Nay, it's not," said Gabrielle shaking her head furiously as tears streamed from her eyes. Her face looked pale and lifeless, and it frightened Annalyse. "I am cursed and God is making me pay for what I did to you, Annalyse. I am so sorry; please forgive me."

Annalyse couldn't forgive her sister just yet and shook her head, remaining silent.

"Someone take this baby, there's another one

coming," said the midwife and Annalyse froze.

"A – a third baby?" she asked in disbelief. When a woman birthed more than one baby at a time, it was believed that they had made love to more than one man. What would the king think? What would her father think? This was awful. And how were they going to hide two babies instead of just one?

"Take it," said the midwife. Annalyse stepped forward and took the squalling baby into her hands. His eyes were wide open and it felt eerie since babies usually had their eyes closed at birth as far as she knew. Bright blue eyes like a bird stared up at her and she felt her sister's pain down to her core now. It was so intense she would have fallen over if Ross hadn't come up behind her and guided her to a chair.

"Sit down, my lady," he told her. She was too frightened to respond.

"The third one is stuck," said the midwife. "Push, my lady. Push hard."

Gabrielle pushed with all her might and even more blood stained the sheets, although Annalyse didn't think it was possible. It looked like a battlefield after a war and she felt as if she were about to retch.

"She's losing too much blood," cried her mother. "Someone, do something!"

"We can't do anything until this baby is born," shouted the midwife. "I can't get it out because it is too big."

"Allow me to help," said Ross, taking off his weapon

belt and rolling up his sleeves. He went to the midwife's aid and was able to help her remove the third and final baby.

"Och, this one looks Scottish," said Ross, cradling the baby in his arms. "He has a full head of red hair, just like me."

"They all have blue eyes, just like my daughters," said her mother.

"Let . . . me hold . . . them," said Gabrielle, too weak to lift her hands up to take them to her bosom.

They brought the three babies over to her. Though her face was pale and she looked close to death, she managed to smile.

"Will you name one of them after King Edward?" asked her mother, running her hand through Gabrielle's hair.

"Nay," said Gabrielle in a soft voice. "These triplets are special. They will have names that will someday be legendary."

"What will you call them?" asked Annalyse.

"The blond one is Rowen," she said, running a hand over the boy's head.

"Like the pagan tree of the Druids?" asked Ross in surprise.

"The rowan tree guards against evil," said Gabrielle, seeming to get more life from holding her children. "This one will be guarded against all evil and watched over by God since he is my first-born son."

"What about the one with the black hair?" asked

Annalyse, pointing to the baby she'd just held. "He looks dark and mysterious."

"Then he shall be called Rook," said Gabrielle with a smile.

"Rook?" asked her mother. "Like the bird?"

"Yes, just like the bird," said Gabrielle. "He is dark and dangerous; I see it in his eyes. But legends say the rook can carry the soul of the dead to the next world. I hope my son can do that for me since I am about to leave this world."

"You're not dying," said Annalyse, looking over to the midwife who was doing everything she could, but the bleeding would not stop. "What about the third born?" she asked, trying to focus on the babies instead of Gabrielle's condition. She felt drained and tired and knew she was picking up the feelings of her sister. There was no doubt Gabrielle's life was slipping away.

"That third baby tore you apart," said the midwife under her breath.

"They all did," answered Gabrielle, kissing the redheaded baby on the cheek. "He won't be blamed for my death and I want you all to make sure he knows that."

"You're not going to die," said Annalyse with tears in her eyes, but she saw the midwife shaking her head. It didn't look promising for Gabrielle.

"This one is Red. What is the Scottish word for red?" Gabrielle's face showed joy and happiness as she cuddled with her newborns, though she could barely speak above a whisper.

"Reid," answered Ross.

"Then he'll be called Reed - but like the reed you'd find in a lake. He will sway in the breeze and change with the times, and nothing will ever stop him."

There was commotion from out in the courtyard and Annalyse ran to look out the open window. Her stomach lurched when she saw King Edward, his queen, and his entourage entering the castle courtyard with her father rushing over to greet them. This was the last thing they needed right now.

"Nay," she said, running back to the others. "The king is here, Gabrielle. What are we going to do? Shall we hide two of the babies?"

Gabrielle's eyes started to close. Holding all three of her sons on her chest, the boys were content and did not cry at all.

"Nay, we will not pretend that two of them don't exist," she whispered.

"But the king and our father will not like this. We have to take them away," Annalyse tried to convince her.

"The king will consider this a bad omen," said their mother with a look of fear in her eyes. "There is no telling what he might do."

"Then we need to protect my babies," muttered Gabrielle, looking even paler than before. Her eyes interlocked with Annalyse's and a pain shot through Annalyse's heart because she felt her sister's life slipping away quickly. "You take them – all of them and raise them for me."

"Me?" Annalyse's heart skipped a beat. "I live in an abbey. I can't take your babies, Gabrielle. Besides, you will want to raise your children yourself."

"Sister, I will only be able to die in peace if you promise me you'll take my sons and keep them safe and treat them as your own."

"I can't," Annalyse protested, feeling more frightened than she ever had in her life. "Don't ask me to do such a thing, because you're not going to die."

"We . . . all know I am . . . dying," whispered Gabrielle. "You can feel it, too. I know you can, since you're my twin."

Annalyse could feel it. And it pained her more than any of the treatment she'd gotten for being the cursed twin through the years. Nothing mattered all of a sudden and when Gabrielle died, part of her would die with her sister.

"I will take them and raise them as if they're my own," she promised her sister, squeezing Gabrielle's hand as the tears fell from her eyes. "I love you, Gabrielle, and I forgive you for not telling me the truth about my birth sooner." With that said, she felt as if she'd made peace with her sister. Now, they would be able to part. She had thought she'd be happy to see her sister leave but never thought she'd be leaving in death. This was not at all how she wanted things to end.

"Annalyse, how can you raise her children without a husband?" asked her mother, crying as well.

"I don't know, but I'll manage." Annalyse drank in the image of her sister with her three babies atop her chest, wanting to remember this sight for as long as she lived.

"You'll have a husband . . . you've already dreamed about him," Gabrielle told her, closing her eyes as death was near.

"Nay, don't die," Annalyse cried, leaning close to her sister. "I forgave you, Gabrielle. You don't need to die as the cursed second twin. Please. You need to live."

"Take my children and . . . never tell them the king is their . . . father. Never . . . tell . . . them." Then Gabrielle died with a smile on her face with her three babies atop her chest and in her arms.

"Nay, Gabrielle, wake up! Please don't die." Annalyse wept bitterly. She leaned over and placed kisses against her sister's forehead, but it was too late. Gabrielle had left this world forever and Annalyse was now the only twin.

"What's all this?" came a male voice from across the room. Annalyse looked up to see King Edward and her father standing in the open doorway with their mouths wide open.

Chapter 9

"Your Majesty," said Annalyse's mother with a bow of her head and a curtsy. The midwife and Annalyse did the same. Annalyse's eyes scanned the room, but somehow in the commotion, Ross had disappeared. Her heart sank. She hoped he'd be there to help her through this, but now that Gabrielle had died, she figured he left since there would be no alliance.

"Ernestine, why wasn't I notified that Gabrielle was birthing her baby?" asked her father, making his way into the room.

"Ramsay . . . she's dead," said Ernestine bursting into tears.

"Nay!" he ran to the bed and stopped in his tracks when he noticed the triplets atop Gabrielle's chest.

"I want to see my bastard," said the king, coming to the bedside. Annalyse held her breath as the king looked down to see the three babies atop her dead sister's chest. "Bid the devil, I am cursed," he spat.

"No, you're not cursed, Your Majesty." Annalyse's father shot her a daggered look. "I'm sure these aren't all your babies."

"Don't lie," growled the king. "I have eyes and can see they are all newborns. And my precious Gabrielle is dead." He reached out and ran a loving hand over Gabrielle's head. A tear dripped down the man's cheek, but he quickly brushed it away.

"This is horrible," said her father, pacing back and forth. The babies all started crying at once and the king did not look happy. "Not only were triplets born on the Feast Day of the Holy Innocents, but my daughter is dead!"

"Your second-born daughter – the real cursed twin," spat Annalyse, feeling angry with her father and only managing to make things worse.

"Lady Gabrielle was a twin?" asked the king, taking a closer look at Annalyse. "Yes, you look just like her. Why was I never told about this?"

"I assure you, it was only because I knew how superstitious you were," blurted out her father. "I didn't see a need to upset you."

"I've had a second-born twin as my mistress and now I have cursed triplets!" Edward bellowed. "How could that not upset me? I've been deceived and I don't like it!"

"Nay, I assure you Gabrielle was the first born," said her father, but the king no longer believed him. King Edward III took one last look at his bastards lying atop his dead mistress' chest and just shook his head.

"I will not have this curse upon me. The bastards will only bring me ill luck."

"What do you mean?" asked Annalyse's mother, still

at Gabrielle's side, tears streaming from her eyes.

"Say your goodbyes to the babies," spat the king. "I will be back with my henchman because the bastards must die."

"Die?" gasped Annalyse. "You're going to kill them? Nay, you can't kill innocent children."

"They aren't innocent, they are birthed by a second-born cursed twin and sent by the devil," growled the king.

"But they're your bastards, Sire," said Ramsay. "Surely you wouldn't kill three sons of your own blood?" He faked a laugh and Annalyse saw him falling apart but felt no remorse for her father.

"I've been deceived," said the king again. "You should feel lucky I'm not ordering your head on a platter, Granville. And look at those bastards. They all have the same face and eyes, but each of them has different colored hair. Aye, they are spawns of the devil, not of my blood, and I will never claim them as my own."

"But the first-born isn't cursed," said her mother, trying to make things better. "Surely, you'll want to claim at least one of your sons?"

"Which one is the first-born?" asked the king, sounding for a minute as if he were considering saving at least one of the babies.

Annalyse's eyes met with her mother's and then the midwife's, but none of them said a word. To save one of the children would be condemning the other two to death. They all knew Rowen was the first-born son, but Annalyse wouldn't tell him and it didn't look like her mother or the midwife would, either.

"Which one is it?" asked the king again.

"I – I'm not sure," said her mother.

"I don't remember, either," said Annalyse. "It all happened so fast."

"Midwife, certainly you'll know since you delivered them," spat the king. "Which one is it?"

Annalyse held her breath, hoping the midwife wouldn't say a word. But the woman had already declared she would never keep such a secret again.

"They all were covered with blood and looked the same. I do not know, Sire," said the midwife keeping her eyes downward.

Annalyse let out the breath she'd been holding, thinking since Edward didn't know the answer, he would let them all live rather than to kill off his first-born son. However, the king was not such a generous man.

"If no one can tell me, then they will all die," he said.

"Sire, these are my grandchildren," said her father. "And I've just lost my daughter, as well. Please, don't do this to me."

"They must die or I know they will be trouble and eventually bring a curse upon my head. I can't have that," stated Edward. "I'm sorry, but my mind is made up and no one will question my decision. My henchman will return to take the lives of the cursed babies."

He headed toward the door and Annalyse's father ran after him. "Please, Sire, let us have a tankard of ale and discuss this."

"There is naught to discuss," said the king, heading down the corridor with Ramsay following at his heels. "The three bastards will be killed and buried along with their deceiving mother."

"Nay!" shouted Annalyse, running to the babies and collecting one in her arms. Her mother and the midwife did the same. "We have to think of something. I promised Gabrielle I'd take care of her babies. I can't let the king kill them."

"You have no choice," said the midwife rocking a crying baby in her arms. "The king has given an order and none of us can change his command."

"I can," came a female voice from the door. Annalyse spun around to see Queen Philippa standing in the doorway with two of her guards behind her. "Leave me," the queen told her guards and walked into the room. When she did, she gasped in surprise as Ross walked out from behind the door and closed it.

"A Scot!" cried the queen. Annalyse knew she had to stop the queen before she called for her guards.

"It's all right, he's a friend," Annalyse told her, walking to Ross with little Rowen in her arms.

"This is Ross of Clan Douglas and he is here by our invitation," she lied.

"Your Majesty," said Ross, bowing his head.

"What were you doing hiding behind the door?" asked the queen, looking as if she'd call for her guards after all.

"I wasna sure if yer husband would take kindly to my alliance with Lord Granville, so I stayed silent and hidden when he entered the room," said Ross.

"Your alliance?" asked the queen suspiciously.

"We are betrothed," Annalyse said without thinking. She noticed the surprised look on Ross' face.

"Actually, that's no' exactly right," said Ross. Annalyse held her breath, hoping he wasn't going to tell the queen the truth. "Lord Ramsay Granville insisted we get married today and so we did."

"Yes, that is true," said Annalyse, knowing it wasn't all a lie.

"On the Feast Day of the Holy Innocents?" asked the queen with a raised brow.

"It was a mock wedding, but my father insisted we practice," Annalyse told the queen, as that is what happened.

"Well, congratulations," said the queen. "Now, we need to talk about these babies before my husband sends his henchman to the chamber."

She swooped across the floor with her long, green velvet gown brushing against the rushes. Queen Philippa was a vision of beauty with her dainty, regal features and her dark hair coiled around each ear. She wore jewels around her neck and rings on her fingers. On her head was a crown made of silver and gold.

"I made a promise to my twin sister that I would raise her babies for her," admitted Annalyse. "But the king thinks his bastards are cursed and will bring him trouble. He's ordered them all killed."

"So I've heard." Philippa looked over to each of the

babies in turn, stretching her neck to see them without getting close to the birthing bed or the blood-stained sheets. Her eyes then settled on Gabrielle and she walked closer to survey her with a wave of sadness covering her face. "I don't approve of my husband's mistresses. However, I was friends with Gabrielle. She was my lady-in-waiting and served me well. I will respect her wishes of having you, her twin sister, raise her children."

"My name is Lady Annalyse," she said, with a bow of the head and another curtsy.

"You look just like Gabrielle," said the queen. "I will miss her dearly."

"My good queen, is there any way you can help us?" asked Annalyse.

"I'm the queen! Of course, I can help you. I don't care what Edward thinks, I am not afraid of curses and silly superstitions. I believe no baby should be killed. Edward is acting no better than Herod and I won't let Gabrielle's babies die by his hand."

"Oh, thank you," wept Annalyse's mother.

"I will also ensure the king does nothing to harm any of your family over this decision, either. But you must take the babies and hide where Edward cannot find you."

"He will come after them," said Annalyse. "How can we outrun a king and his army?"

"He won't come after you if he thinks his bastards are dead."

"You're going to lie to your husband?" asked Ernestine.

"Hasn't he lied enough to me? Edward's henchman has done favors for me in the past and I will pay him well to keep the secret. I will tell Edward I oversaw the deaths of the babies and he will think I did it out of jealousy. Lady Annalyse, take the children and hide in the hills. Go across the border to Scotland to raise them where Edward won't find you."

"Across the border? By myself?" Annalyse was horrified even to think of such a thing.

"I'll go with you," offered the midwife. "I'll help you raise the children. It is the least I can do to make up for keeping a secret I should never have kept."

"Thank you, Midwife, but I don't believe two women and three babies will be safe traveling alone," Annalyse answered.

"You'll have your betrothed with you to protect all of you," said the queen and Ross stepped forward.

"Aye. Ye willna be alone, Lady Annalyse, as I will be with ye as well as my brother and two others of my clan as we travel back to Scotland. Ye will come to live with Clan Douglas as my wife, and we will raise yer sister's babies as our own."

"Ross?" asked Annalyse, her eyes darting from him to her mother, then to the midwife and back to him again. "What are you saying?"

"I ken our marriage was a mock marriage today, Annalyse. But as soon as we get to Scotland, we will be married for real. That is what ye want, isna it?"

"Why, yes, I suppose so," she said, feeling a swarm of

emotions travel through her. She cuddled the baby to her chest and looked over to her dead sister on the bed and tears escaped her eyes. "Would you really agree to raise the English king's bastards as your own?"

"I ken what it means to ye to keep yer promise to yer sister," he said, putting his hand on Annalyse's shoulder. "Aye, my lady, I agree. Rowen, Rook, and Reed will be our sons from this day on."

"Good, then hurry, as you must leave now," said the queen. "I will keep my husband distracted while you go to the stables and get a cart for your travels."

"Thank you, Queen Philippa," said Annalyse's mother, kissing Reed and handing the baby to Ross. "I will tell no one what you've done for us this day."

"Not even your husband," the queen warned. "If he knows, it'll only endanger him if the king ever discovers the truth."

The midwife took Rook. Annalyse hugged and kissed her mother goodbye.

"Thank ye, Yer Highness," said Ross with a bow to the queen. "Yer kindness is appreciated."

"I will leave the room first and take my guards' attention," said the queen. "As soon as I'm down the corridor, you must all hurry to the stable and leave." The queen left the room and Annalyse's mother took two cloaks from hooks on the wall and placed them over the midwife's and Annalyse's shoulders.

"Take good care of my daughter and my grandsons," she said to Ross. "This might be the last I ever see them."

"Nay, Mother," said Annalyse. "I'll return again someday, I promise."

"Come, Annalyse, we must hurry," said Ross, leading the way to the door.

"Wait!" Annalyse ran back to her sister, holding the baby securely. She bent down and kissed Gabrielle goodbye, feeling no more pain from her twin. "Goodbye, Gabrielle. I hope you are in a far better place now. I promised you I would raise your sons and keep the truth of who sired them from the boys. That is what I'll do. I love you, no matter what happened between us, and I forgive you." She looked up to her mother. "I forgive you all."

"Come on, lassie," said Ross, putting his arm around her and guiding her to the door. Annalyse was leaving for Scotland, now a mother and about to be a bride. Her life was about to change forever. She looked back at her mother who was crying at Gabrielle's side and realized that she and her twin sister would always be close, even in death. Gabrielle would live on through Rowen, Rook, and Reed - the king's bastards.

Chapter 10

Lowlands, Scotland

Annalyse stood next to her husband with the baby, Rowen, in her arms, a few days later, looking out over the vast, wide open space occupied by Clan Douglas. She and Ross had married as soon as they'd arrived. Although the clan accepted them, she picked up their fear from seeing the triplets. She'd told the clan the babies belonged to her departed sister but didn't breathe a word of them being King Edward's bastards.

Her marriage to Ross was bittersweet. While she was happy to be out of the abbey and even more elated to be married to such a kind and handsome man, she missed her family dearly – especially her sister.

"Och, Wife, why dinna ye smile? Ye are married now, lassie. Dinna tell me ye are no' happy." Ross held both Rook and Reed in his strong arms and she drank in the glorious sight, since she knew he would make a wonderful father.

"I am happy, Husband," she said, testing the word on her tongue, reaching up and giving him a peck on the cheek. "I am just concerned that the clan will think the triplets are a curse. People have been asking a lot of questions about them. You didn't tell them the truth, did you?"

"Of course no'," said Ross, looking down and smiling at the babies. "They dinna need to ken these are the English king's bastards. I'll raise them as our own and train them to fight and be strong warriors."

"Oh, Ross! Do you mean you are going to teach them to fight against Edward? Somehow that doesn't seem right. He is their father."

"Nay. I'm their faither now, Annalyse, and ye are their mathair. That's all they need to ken for now. When the boys are older and the time is right, then mayhap we can tell them the truth about who sired them."

"Never," she said, shaking her head. Then she looked down at little Rowen who started fussing. "We made a promise to my sister and we will keep it. My mother won't tell a soul and the midwife has agreed to keep the secret as well. Ross, tell me you and your brother and friends who know the truth will keep silent about it, too."

He hesitated and, for a mere second, Annalyse got the feeling that he was having second thoughts. She knew he hated King Edward and how hard it would be to raise the king's bastards as his own. But the boy's needed this chance. They had to do it for them and also for Gabrielle.

Ross had done his best to convince his clan the triplets were not cursed. However, he told Annalyse they needed to keep some distance from everyone, so they'd decided to build a cottage on the outskirts of the clan where they would live with the children and the old midwife.

"The secret is safe and will always be," said Ross, flashing her a smile that melted her heart and made her feel like everything was going to be all right, even if she had an unsettled feeling in her gut that this was all far from over.

"Do you think our meeting was by accident or was it possibly meant to be?" she asked her new husband. "After all, everything happened so fast and we've yet to get to know each other well. I only hope, someday, we can be in love, too, the way Gabrielle loved King Edward."

"I think I loved ye from the moment I first kissed ye under the kissin' bough," he told her. That caused her to feel special. She loved her new life with Ross and would do her best to raise her nephews to make Gabrielle proud.

Annalyse felt free now, feeling no more pain from her sister. It was as if a veil had been lifted and she felt the joy in Gabrielle's heart as she looked at her three new sons. Her sister would always be watching over her children and Annalyse would do her best to keep her promise to her sister to raise the boys as her own and never tell them who sired them. It was better if they didn't know King Edward was their father and wanted them dead. But a part of Annalyse would be sad forever if she couldn't someday tell the boys about their mother.

"I think I'm in love with you, too, Ross. And I'm glad I didn't reject your kiss under the kissing bough or I might have never gotten married."

"Aye," answered Ross. "That kissin' bough does seem to hold a wee bit of magic and I'm glad it brought us together. It was a destined fate, I guess ye could say. Now what do I have to do to get a kiss from my wife?" asked Ross, staring down at her mouth.

"Just ask," she said with a giggle.

"I have a better idea." He shifted both babies to one arm and dug in his sporran and pulled out a sprig of mistletoe and held it up high over her head.

"What are you doing?" she asked, laughing, looking up at the greenery in his hand.

"I'm creatin' that first magical moment again," he said, leaning over and kissing her passionately.

"I love it," she said reaching up and taking the mistletoe from him, twirling it in her fingers. "I never knew when I kissed you under the kissing bough that I'd someday be your wife."

"Aye," he answered. "One kiss under the kissin' bough planned our entire future. I guess ye could say it was ***Destiny's Kiss***!"

From the Author:

I hope you enjoyed Annalyse and Ross' story. I incorporated legends, superstitions, and traditions of the time into the story to bring history to my readers. I found the times fascinating, as well as the legends of the kissing bough. Bringing ivy indoors meant death and if one made a wish when they ate mince pie at Christmas, their wish would come true. The customs and superstitions of the Feast Day of the Holy Innocents were taken from history and woven into my story to make it more authentic.

Back in medieval times, the second-born twin was considered cursed and people thought this was the work of the devil. Just think what would have happened if they saw triplets!

This is the prequel to my **Legendary Bastards of the Crown Series** and leads into the trilogy about the triplet brothers.

You can read Rowen's story in **Restless Sea Lord – Book 1**. It will be followed by Rook's story, **Ruthless Knight – Book 2**, and Reed's story, **Reckless Highlander – Book 3**. At the end of Book 3 the follow-up to Annalyse and Ross' story will be told as well.

I usually overlap characters from my series, such as *Storm MacKeefe* who makes an appearance in *Restless Sea Lord*. You can read his story in **Lady Renegade –**

Book 2 of my **Legacy of the Blade Series**.

Please make sure to stop by and visit my website at **http://elizabethrosenovels.com** to find out more about my books. You can also follow me on Twitter **@ElizRoseNovels**, or Facebook, **Elizabeth Rose – Author**, (don't forget the dash.)

Elizabeth Rose

Excerpt from Restless Sea Lord – Book 1
(Legendary Bastards of the Crown Series)

"I'm on my way." Rowen walked around the corner of the building and when he did, he thought he saw movement in the shadows. Someone had been eavesdropping on their conversation and was hiding behind the rain barrel.

He ripped his sword from his side, reaching around the barrel with his free hand, and yanked the eavesdropper out into the open. He planned on slitting the man's throat but stopped when he felt the small size of his arms. The sneak's hood fell back revealing his face. Rowen swore under his breath when he realized it wasn't a man at all but rather the witch lady from inside the tavern.

"Damn you!" he spat. "How long have you been hiding there?" He'd been so distracted by thoughts of his sister that he hadn't even noticed the wench had followed him. This wasn't good. If she'd heard their entire conversation, she could ruin everything.

"Let me go, Rowen the Restless," she said, struggling in his grip.

"You know who I am?"

"I didn't need to hear you and your brothers to figure it out. I saw your birds."

Damn. Rowen knew those birds were going to give them trouble someday. His brothers had been way too careless. "You know too much," he growled.

"Lady Cordelia, are you back here?" Her guard came around the corner. Just when Rowen was sure she was going to shout out, he did the only thing he could to shut her up. He pulled her into his arms and covered her mouth with his and kissed her hard.

"Lady Cordelia?" asked the guard, stopping in his tracks. "Are you all right?"

Rowen heard the sound of shouting and the war cries of his brothers and their armies, realizing the fools must have thought his kissing the wench was the signal to attack. Well, now that the plan was in action, he had no choice but to join them in their ploy.

Spinning on his heel, he hit the guard in the head with the hilt of his sword, sending the man sprawling on the ground.

"Nay!" Cordelia cried out. Rowen pulled her out of the way as a dagger whizzed past her ear and embedded itself into the rain barrel. Water spouted out, hitting the guard in the face. The man's eyes opened and he sputtered, hurrying to get to his knees.

"God's eyes, I don't have time to protect you now," Rowen said, kicking the sword out of the guard's hand and then turning around to meet one of the king's soldiers head on. Swiping his sword forward, he sank it into the soldier's chest before the man could do the same to him. Cordelia screamed at seeing all the blood. She was going to ruin everything! "Keep your mouth shut unless you want to lose your head," he warned, this time blocking her with his body as his brother, Reed, tossed a guard through the air. The man landed at their feet, and Cordelia peeked out from behind him and screamed again.

"Sorry about that," called out Reed. "I didna see the lassie there."

"You've got a girl?" shouted Rook, taking down two guards with ease. "This isn't the time for that, you fool. Do something with her."

"Just do your job and get the guards away from the cart and let me worry about the wench," he spat, seeing a soldier running toward him with his sword drawn. Dressed the way she was, looking like an old hag, no one was going to think a noblewoman was right in the midst of the battle. And they wouldn't care if a peasant was killed in the fight.

Brody climbed into the driver's seat of the cart and waved his arm through the air to get Rowen's attention, while his brothers kept the rest of the soldiers at bay. They had to leave now if they were to have any chance at all of getting the goods to the ship and away from the coast without being caught.

"Go," he shouted, signaling Brody who slapped the reins and started the horses moving forward. The battle was still in full swing and he couldn't just leave the wench there unprotected. Besides, she'd heard too much. With one word from her, their operation could be blown apart. He had no choice but to take her with him.

"Let me go," she cried out as he pulled her by the arm toward the approaching cart. When Brody passed by with the goods, Rowen tossed her into the back of the wagon.

Managing to fight off another soldier, he then jumped up into the cart with her. They sped away toward the Sea Mirage, with Rowen wondering how he was going to explain this one to his brothers and his crew.

Made in the USA
Middletown, DE
02 April 2018